SURRENDER OF THE BRUTAL KING

THE POSEIDON TRIALS

ELIZA RAINE

ROSE WILSON

You're not broken.
You just haven't found what brings you to life yet...

ALMI

Freezing water engulfed me before it even occurred to me to swallow some water-root. If I was being honest, *nothing* had fully occurred to me before leaping on the pegasus' back and diving in after Poseidon's sinking form.

Blue beat his wings on either side of me, and we powered through the water faster than I ever could have managed on my own. But Poseidon's stone body was sinking faster.

I gripped Blue's mane, panic and fear flooding my system, and no idea at all what I would even do if I could reach him before I ran out of air.

Blue must have sensed my thoughts because he surged forward suddenly, spurring us farther into the darkening depths. Poseidon's armor glinted in the now dusky light, and a bolt of hope made my muscles tighten as I realized we were now moving faster than he was. Barely ten seconds later, the pegasus had caught him up, his golden wings cutting through the ocean currents as he swooped beneath the sinking god. I shifted on Blue's back and clung on as Poseidon's heavy form landed hard across the winged horse's shoulders. He began to slide, and I wrapped one arm tight around him as I tried to grip Blue harder with my thighs.

The pegasus kicked his way up, his load now significantly heavier and his pace reflecting it. I tried not to notice the burn in my lungs, or the ice cold feel of Poseidon's chest under my unsteady grip.

What the hell had happened? Had the healer's magic worn off? Had killing that insane creature weakened him enough the stone took over?

And what the hell would I do with him when we got to the surface?

If we got to the surface.

Blue's wings beat even harder as he struggled, and the exertion required for me to keep the statue of Poseidon on the pegasus's back and hang on myself was exhausting. I would run out of air soon, I knew.

A voice rang through my mind, tense and urgent. *Just get him to the finish line. We can't interfere until the Trial is over, but we can help as soon as you're back.*

Persephone?

Had she and the other gods seen what had happened? Could they see us now?

Willing the pegasus to move faster, I craned my neck to look up. Light shone above the surface of the water, and blessed air was so close now. My lips parted, and I clamped them closed again.

Come on, come on, come on, please. Please, let me hold my breath a little longer.

It wasn't just my life dependent on my ability to survive. It was Lily's and Poseidon's, too.

A tiny stream of bubbles corkscrewed through the water toward me, growing larger as it got closer, and I tensed. Poseidon slipped in my grasp, and I was forced to let go of Blue's mane to grab him, lifting him tighter between my body and the pegasus' neck. The motion was too much, and my lungs burned like they were filled with acid. My mouth opened, my nostrils filling with water as instinct forced me to try to suck in air.

The ribbon of bubbles rushed me, zooming around my head and pouring into my mouth. Air, cool and crisp, filled my throat and lungs, and I gasped. Relief slammed through me as the bubbles kept whizzing, lifting my hair from my stinging eyes and making my vision clearer as they delivered blessed air into my body.

I had no idea where the air was coming from, but I sent a prayer of thanks to whoever had heard my plea as I gulped it down.

The bubbles rushed around my head, so fast that they blurred together, making a layer of clear air all around my face, as though I was wearing a helmet of air. I adjusted my grip on Blue, rubbing his shoulder encouragingly, and I heard a faint whinny through the water. I tried speaking, my thoughts singular, exhaustion and desperation forcing adrenaline through my body.

"You're doing fucking amazing, Blue. You're saving his life." My voice came out clearly. I blinked incredulously as the pegasus whinnied louder, and I was sure he moved a little faster.

Seconds later, my head broke through the surface. The

bubbles vanished, and I twisted in my awkward position to see the Crosswind right next to us.

Finish the race, I told myself urgently.

I had to finish the race.

Blue kept beating his wings, and it pained me to see how tired he was. "Can you get us to the ship?" He gave a small, exhausted whinny, then he lifted us from the sea.

I suppressed a shriek as Poseidon's stone body began to slip again, but Blue moved fast, and within another few seconds we were hovering next to the box that moved up and down to the bridge. Scrambling, I tipped the Poseidon statue into the crate and climbed in after him. Free of his heavy burden, Blue shook his wings, his legs kicking in the air.

"Thank you," I breathed. "See you on deck."

I willed the box to rise, unable to pull the door shut with Poseidon lying there, limbs unmovable. I looked at the expression etched into his beautiful face as I slumped against the wood, panting.

Sadness. His expression was one of almost unbearable sadness.

Why in the name of all the gods had I gone in after him?

What the frigging hell had I been thinking?

I hadn't, I realized. Rational thought had abandoned me utterly, instinct as deep as my soul sending me into the sea.

Had he made me do it, before he had turned to stone? Had he compelled me to save him with magic? I was the only one who could have helped him; only the competitors could be involved in the Trial.

The box clacked as it reached the deck, and I dragged

myself to my feet as fast as I could, pulling Poseidon's insanely heavy stone body with me as I moved onto the deck. His stone boots left scratches on the planks.

"I'm sorry, ship," I told her as I let go of him and jogged to the wheel. "Take me to the finish line, please."

Blue touched down on the deck as Kryvo squeaked, and the ship lurched forward.

"Almi! Almi, I thought you were dead! You can't be dead, you're my only friend!"

"I'm not dead," I assured him, pushing my wet hair back from my face and gratefully breathing in the ocean air in long breaths.

"Is Poseidon?"

I glanced over my shoulder at his solid granite body. "No. Not yet."

2

ALMI

The second the Crosswind sailed over the gleaming finish line, there was a flash of white light, and Hades and Persephone appeared on the deck beside me. Persephone moved to Poseidon's side in an instant, vines shooting from her palms and wrapping around Poseidon's limbs before she even reached him.

"What happened to him?" Hades asked, turning to me. An overwhelming urge to bow to the god of the dead took me, and his silver eyes swirled as his gaze bore into mine.

Atlas' voice boomed through the sky before I could answer, glee in his voice.

"It seems we may have suffered a casualty in the Poseidon Trials already!"

Hades' face twisted into a snarl and tendrils of smoke leaked from his body, obscuring his black clothing.

"Hades, I can't wake him, but he's alive in there."

We both turned at Persephone's voice.

Somehow, I had already known he was still alive, but

that didn't stop the relief I felt at having my instincts confirmed.

Hades turned back to me. "What happened?" he repeated.

"I don't know. I mean, I know he has been fighting an affliction that turns people to stone." There was no point hiding that from them anymore. "But I don't know why it happened now. Were you watching?"

Hades nodded slowly, looking between me and the stone god. "Yes. The whole thing is being broadcast in the flame dishes." Flame dishes were like TVs in Olympus. Most households had large iron bowls to keep burning embers in, so they could gather round and watch whatever the gods wanted to show the world.

"Why was he fighting that monster?"

"Atlas," Hades growled. "The creature was waiting for Poseidon. It let Kalypso and Ceto straight over the finish line without even surfacing. As soon as Poseidon got there, it rose up, dragging him and his ship under. Polybotes crossed just before you reached the finish-line and had no attention from the beast whatsoever. It was only after my brother."

"We need to find someone who can help him," Persephone said, standing up from where she was crouched over Poseidon.

"He said a healer had been helping him keep it at bay, but they couldn't cure it."

"What healer?"

I frowned as I answered. "He didn't say, but Galatea is the only other person who knew about this."

"Then we'll ask her. Are you ready to go?" Hades

looked at me, and I was so unaccustomed to being asked if I was ready for something, that I just blinked at him.

Persephone spoke softly. "I can understand you might be in shock, Almi. But we must go now."

I shook my head. "Wait!" I turned back to the ship's wheel. Kryvo flashed red just long enough that I could see where he was hiding. "Thank you, ship," I said loudly, trying to mask the fact I was lifting the little starfish into my palm. "Okay. I'm ready."

We flashed into the courtyard of the palace, where Galatea and a dozen palace staff and guards were standing before an enormous flame dish, an image of the finish line and the four surviving ships hovering in the orange flames.

"Sire." She rushed forward, her face a mask of horror.

"Galatea, who was the healer who helped him before?"

She turned to me, and instead of anger or suspicion, I was shocked to see her expression was one of pure gratitude. "You saved him. He would be lying on the ocean floor right now, if it weren't for you."

"I, erm…" I ran one hand through my tangled hair awkwardly. "Blue helped, too," I said.

She reached out, clasping my other hand. "Thank you."

Hades sighed. "The healer," he commanded. "Now."

Galatea turned to him, her face flushing and her head bowing low. "Of course, mighty one."

Shit, should I have been calling him that? I glanced at Persephone, and she gave me a tiny smile of reassurance.

"It was a dragon, on the realm of Pisces. She does not take visitors lightly."

A dragon? I gaped at Galatea.

Hades nodded. "Erimítis?"

"Yes," confirmed Galatea. "She will only entertain one as strong as you or your brothers."

"Fine. I will take Poseidon to her myself." Hades turned to Persephone, kissing her with an intensity I didn't know was possible in such a brief embrace. "I will see you as soon as I can, my love."

"Be safe," she said, touching his cheek. There was a flash, and the two brothers were gone.

Persephone looked at me as I blinked around dazedly.

"You look like you could do with a sit down," she said. "And maybe a stiff drink."

When I looked at her, the feeling of warmth she generated in me was so unfamiliar that I was tempted to distrust it. But she was a healer, and she appeared to harbor no animosity toward me. Maybe she was just... being nice.

I felt a flash of desire to call up Lily's image, to be alone with her so I could go through everything that had just happened. But then I would have to face up to a whole load of questions. *Like why the hell I had risked my life and hers to save Poseidon's.*

"A drink sounds good." Putting those questions off a while longer suited me just fine. "If there are donuts, that would be even better."

"If you need donuts, I can find donuts," said Galatea, still looking at me like I was some sort of hero.

"Seriously? You can get me donuts?"

"I will get you whatever you want. You saved the king."

Her words rolled around in my head as I followed her and Persephone into the palace, discreetly lifting

Kryvo to my collarbone when the women's backs were turned.

You saved the king.

Why? Why had I saved him?

I couldn't avoid the damned question.

And deep down, I knew I couldn't avoid the answer, either.

I could have told myself that it was because Poseidon had spent the entire time I'd been caught up in this obscene mess saving my life. I owed him.

I could have told myself it was because I believed him to be the right person to rule Aquarius, and that ancient angry Titans were the bad guys and I was obligated to keep the true king on the throne.

I could have told myself that it was because I was the only one who could have helped him at that point, and I wasn't wired to let a person die when I could stop it from happening.

The truth, though?

I couldn't *not* have gone in after him. It wasn't something I had carefully thought through and come to a sensible decision on. Leaping into the ocean after him had been as instinctive as walking, or even breathing.

I may have barely known the man, but I was connected to him somehow. His fiery temper and miserable attitude were the antithesis of the light and bright Lily, and he represented everything I didn't want in my life — control, rules, and sullen silence.

Yet, when I looked into those stormy eyes, I could feel the passion he was suppressing. I didn't know what the passion was for; perhaps that endless sense of freedom I had felt from him more than once, or the bond he had with the creatures of his realm? But whatever it was, I knew there was more to the fierce and controlled god of the sea than what he was presenting to the world.

And if I hadn't been certain?

Then that smile… *Fuck, that smile.*

I wished I'd never seen it. So brief, and yet I needed to see it again.

And I hadn't needed anything other than my sister, my whole life.

3

ALMI

The emotions and thoughts fighting for attention inside me were bordering on overwhelming. I rubbed my hand across my face.

"Shit, sorry!" I'd been so distracted I'd walked straight into Persephone.

"You okay?" She steadied me as Galatea pulled open the large double doors on our left.

"Sure. A bit… overwhelmed," I said.

"I know the feeling."

Persephone ushered me into the room after Galatea, and a weird calm came over me as I entered the space.

Not a foggy calm, like the demon jackass angler fish had caused, but a serene, relaxing vibe that made me want to curl up with a good book and doze peacefully.

"We call this the drawing-room," said Galatea. "I'm sure Poseidon won't mind us using it while you recover."

I associated the idea of a drawing-room with English period dramas, and in some ways, I could kind of make the connection. It looked like the room was half of one tower, a semi-circle in shape. There were walls between the columns ringing the edge of the room, but huge drapes lined them, almost like tapestries. The fabric was exactly like the stuff Poseidon's robe was made from, and though the material didn't move, the colors of the ocean swirled and played across the surface.

The floor wasn't covered in marble tiles like everywhere else I'd seen in the palace, but a rich, soft, black carpet instead. Huge squishy couches were dotted around the room in various shades of navy, and rosewood side tables covered in books and trinkets stood beside the chairs. Tall potted plants at random intervals along the walls gave it a slightly exotic air, and I was sure I could hear the gentle lapping of waves.

"It's lovely," Persephone said, running her fingers through the leaves of a ten-foot-tall bamboo plant as she walked along the edge of the room.

"It is," I nodded. "Very relaxed."

Persephone glanced at me. "Unlike your husband."

I snorted, and she smiled as she picked a couch big enough for three and sat down. She was wearing jeans and a green wraparound top, her long white hair tied back in a complicated braid. Her bottom half said human world, and her top half said Olympus. She patted the cushion beside her, and I made my decision.

I was going to trust her.

"So, donuts, and what do you want to drink?" Galatea asked as I moved to the couch.

"I'll have red wine, please," said Persephone. "Dionysus knows his shit," she added to me.

"Then I'll join you."

I didn't really drink red wine, ever. I was more of a beer-if-I-could-afford-it kind of girl. But who was I to turn down wine made by a god?

"Be right back." Galatea strode from the room.

"You must be worried," Persephone said. I shifted on the couch so I could see her face.

"Okay. Here's the thing. No. But yes. And I shouldn't be."

Her pretty brows drew together. "I don't follow you."

I blew out a sigh. "That makes two of us."

Galatea came back into the room and sat down in an armchair facing our couch. "This dragon," she said. "She will help the king. She did before, and she will again, I am sure." Tense concern was etched into Galatea's face.

"Poseidon will be fine," I said.

"How do you know?"

"Because… I do."

"Your marriage bond," said Persephone, knowingly. "I always know if Hades is in trouble."

"Erm, about that. You see, I am technically Poseidon's wife, but it was a very quick wedding, and then he hid me in the human world where nobody could find me for-" I glanced at Galatea apologetically. "Eight years."

Persephone's lips parted in surprise. "What made you return?"

Galatea moved forward in her seat, and I realized she would be keen to know the true answer to this question too.

"My sister," I said. It was the truth, and I had no intention of giving either woman details of how I got back, or my plan to find Atlantis.

"You said she was sick?"

"Yes. Eight years ago, she fell unconscious. Since I returned, I discovered that she has an ailment that is turning her to stone."

Persephone frowned. "Is she connected to Poseidon and his ailment?"

I shrugged. "I don't know." I looked at Galatea, unsure how much to say about the blight that was spreading through Aquarius. "Atlas referred to me as the last of the Nereids, but he's wrong. Lily lives."

"What has that got to do with the stone?"

I sighed again. There was a knock on the door, and a nymph entered with a tray laden with three glasses of ruby-red wine and a huge plate of donuts.

When we each had a drink and I'd practically inhaled a salted caramel delight, I continued.

"The Oracle at Delphi told Poseidon that something called the heart of the ocean is the only way to cure the blight. And... The only way to possess the heart of the ocean is to possess the heart of a Nereid."

Persephone looked at me a long moment, then took a deep drink of her wine.

I decided to do the same. "Fuck, that's tasty," I muttered.

"So Poseidon married you for this heart of the ocean?"

"Yeah. Then he hid me, so nobody could steal me from him."

"What a prick," she murmured.

"Yes!" I exclaimed, as Galatea tutted loudly. "But anyway, it didn't work. He doesn't have his heart of the ocean." I took one more massive breath and turned square on to Galatea. "I may as well tell you this. Poseidon knows already, and… Well it's probably just easier that you know."

She looked at me warily. "What?"

"I'm broken." I swallowed, then took another big gulp of delicious wine. "I have no power. The nautilus shell tattoo of a Nereid should be filled with color, like my sister's. My hair should be bright blue and my skin shiny like pearls."

I took another swig of wine, and realized I had never said those words out loud before.

"I should be able to control water, to long to be in it, to have an affinity with the ocean. I don't. I can't do anything with it. I can't even hold my breath longer than a human."

It was as though I was letting out over two decades of a dirty secret, and I couldn't stop.

"My sister went to the academy, and she was amazing. Her water magic rivaled a god's. That's who Poseidon was supposed to marry to get his heart of the ocean." I let out a long breath. "He married the wrong sister."

Galatea blinked at me, then drained her own glass. "You have no magic," she repeated.

"Uh-uh."

"And you survived the first Trial?"

That wasn't what I had expected her to say. I nodded. "Yeah. With help. Poseidon spoke to me when that fish lured me in, and he saved me from the storm."

"Almi, the fact that you even showed up with no magic is insane!"

"It's not like I had much choice," I mumbled.

"I admire your bravery. Both in the Trials and in telling us this now."

"You… You do?" I had never been admired before.

"Yes. But we do now have a massive problem."

"Yes, we do," said Persephone. "If the only way to wake your sister up is with the heart of the ocean, and the only way to get it is for Poseidon to marry her…"

"Can you marry an unconscious person?"

"No. I'm pretty sure that's not a thing."

"Shit."

Galatea stood and topped up our wine glasses from a tall bottle that looked no emptier than when she had started.

"Can we awaken your powers somehow?" Persephone asked hopefully.

"I can't tell you how much I would love that. But I wouldn't know where to start. Lily could never get them to show."

"What is the heart of the ocean anyway? Didn't the little old lady throw it into the sea at the end?"

The explosion of warmth I felt for the woman sitting beside me caused me to grip her arm. "You should have seen the look on Poseidon's face when I said the same thing to him," I said.

Persephone snorted as she laughed, then gave a small squeal as she nearly spilled her wine. I couldn't help laughing with her.

"What is funny?" asked Galatea.

Through giggles, we tried to explain the movie Titanic to Galatea. "That sounds like a very sad way to spend three hours," she said.

I nodded. "Yeah. Totally worth it though."

Persephone nodded. "Die-hard romantics don't get it much better."

"I do not have time for romance," Galatea said, a little sadly.

There was a flash of white light that made all of us jump in surprise, then Hades was standing beside the couch.

"Poseidon is resting. He will be fully recovered in a few hours," he said.

"By fully recovered, do you mean-"

Hades shook his head, ending my question before I finished it. "She is not able to cure the blight. As she did before, she can keep it from taking his whole body, but only as long as he does not exert so much power again."

"How is he supposed to win the Trials without exerting power?" asked Galatea, a new expression of concern covering her stern face.

"A very good question. And one I have no answer for."

"When is the next Trial?" asked Persephone.

Hades scowled. "If he knows Poseidon is injured, then Atlas will start it soon, so he has less time to recover."

Nerves fluttered through my gut, and I reached for another donut in an effort to settle my stomach. The thought of facing another Trial...

"Almi."

I turned to Hades as he said my name.

"He asked to see you."

4

ALMI

*P*oseidon was lying in a bed much like the one in my guest room. In fact, the whole room looked very similar to the one I was staying in. But I didn't take much time to check out the decor. My focus was entirely on the god of the ocean.

I found myself moving fast to his bedside, gaze locked on his face. His eyes fluttered open as I reached him, and he moved, sitting up. The sheets fell away from his completely bare chest, and I paused, suddenly awkward.

"Hi," I said, raising a hand, then feeling really stupid.

"You saved me." His serious face burned with rigid control.

"Yeah, I guess. Couldn't have done it without Blue."

"Why?"

I couldn't help a small laugh at the irony of his question. "Now you know how I feel," I said.

His fierce blue eyes softened. "I mean it. I thought nothing was more important than your sister. If you had died trying to save me, then your sister would not be saved either."

A ripple of fear moved through my whole body at the truth of his words.

"You saved me a bunch of times," I said quietly. "I was just returning the favor."

Energy seemed to thrum around the room, and I couldn't help drinking in the rich, tanned tone of his skin, savoring the lack of granite stone. Last time I'd seen him… "I knew you weren't dead," I blurted out. "I don't know how, but I knew you were alive inside the stone."

"I was not conscious," he replied, his lips barely moving.

"How do you know I saved you then?"

"Hades told me. Almi, you are connected to this blight somehow."

"I don't know about that, but I know…" I bit my lip, trying to work out how to say what I was thinking. "I know I am connected to *you* somehow, and you to me. Why else would you have agreed to the Trials to save my life in the first place? And why risk your success in the first Trial to save me from the storm? It's for the same reason I went in after you, isn't it?"

He took a slow breath, chest expanding. I kept my eyes on his. "We have a bond, yes."

"What kind of bond?"

He frowned at me. "I know it was almost a decade ago, but I assume you haven't forgotten us being married in front of Hera?"

I gave him my best scowl back. "Yeah, women forget their wedding days often," I replied sarcastically, fisting my hand on my hip. "You're saying the marriage is what's causing us to want to save each other?" I emphasized the word *save* and hoped it wasn't obvious that, on my part, it could easily have been substituted with a number of other words. Especially when he was shirtless.

"Yes." Emotion flickered in his eyes, too fast for me to decipher.

I was tired, I realized, emotionally and physically, and I decided to change the subject, unwilling and unable to process the notion of marriage bonds. "Can I have some more of those vials before the next Trial, please?"

"Yes. I can't conjure them now. I need to wait for my strength to return."

"Thanks." I bit my lip again.

"Thank you," he said, his voice deep and sincere.

I raised my eyebrows. "You're, erm, welcome."

"Why do you have a starfish on your shoulder?"

I froze. "I don't know what you're talking about." He gave me a look, and I sighed resignedly. "He's my friend." I looked down at my chest. "Kryvo, you've been busted." The starfish remained silent, and camouflaged, but I could feel his warmth on my skin. "I think he's too shy to say hello," I told Poseidon.

"Hades said you were seen talking to someone the whole Trial. Was it the starfish?"

I flushed. It hadn't occurred to me that I was being broadcast. "Yeah."

"Does he talk back?" Poseidon was speaking to me like I was some sort of crazy person, which led me to believe that he didn't know the starfish was part of his own palace. Did that mean he didn't know the starfish could spy on him through the other statues?

Thinking fast, I decided on a partially true answer. "Yes. But he doesn't say much. He's sort of an emotional support starfish."

Poseidon frowned at me. "You are odd. Very, very odd."

"Gotta be odd to be number one," I grinned at him, reciting a favorite mantra.

He shook his head, but I was certain the corner of his mouth quirked up a tiny bit. "I think there is little chance of either of us being number one right now. I am unable to use my full power due to this accursed blight and the loss of my trident. We must come up with a new plan to win these Trials."

"I'm not here to win," I said, shaking my head.

He stared at me a long moment before speaking, and I concentrated on not looking at his nipples. "Then perhaps we can try something different for the next Trial."

"What did you have in mind?"

"If you stay where I can see you, I will not have to worry about rescuing you all the time."

I opened my mouth to defend my sorry ass but closed it again. There was no point. I was so far out of my depth it was laughable. "You're suggesting we work together?"

He nodded. "Under the proviso that you are not in this to steal my trident and realm." A hard glint shone in his eyes, the crashing waves simmering dangerously.

I snorted. "Fuck no. I just want to wake my sister up."

"Then we tackle the next Trial together. Hopefully I will lose less ground, not having to keep an eye on you."

I folded my arms over my chest, unable to take being patronized any more. "Maybe I'll be the one saving you next time."

As if. But I had done it once—I'd milk that for everything it was worth.

One of his brows rose, and he folded his own arms, making his pecs tense. "Stay out of trouble, don't slow me down, and we might stand a chance of you surviving, and me winning," he growled.

POSEIDON

I watched Almi leave, my jaw working as she cast a small glance back over her shoulder at me.

"Fuck," I swore, once she had closed the door behind her.

She was getting too close to the truth. Too close to the real reason I'd had to leave her alone in the human realm for all that time.

But I couldn't beat the blight without her.

I needed her close to me.

ALMI

It was both a relief, and a burden, to be alone in my room at last. I climbed up onto the bed to open the window as soon as I'd set Kryvo on his little cushion.

Slumping onto the pillows, I let out a long breath.

I'd survived.

And now, I had to talk to Lily.

I couldn't escape the fact that something had changed. It wasn't just me and her anymore. Poseidon was linked to me, and I him.

"Lily?" I closed my eyes and sank as far as I could into the pillows behind me.

Almi. Kindness laced the single word as her image appeared in my mind.

"I'm sorry. I risked your life today."

You've been risking your life for me forever. Today you did something for you. I'm pleased.

"Really? In what way was that doing something for me?"

She laughed, the sound tinkling. It made me feel warmer, safer. *You know, you are odd. You faced some of the most terrifying things in this realm today, and you were incredible. You were brave, resourceful, smart... You survived a Trial meant for gods.*

"I guess."

And here you are, only thinking about one thing.

"Poseidon," I said on a sigh.

He is your husband, she said, a playful smile on her lips.

"This doesn't worry you? This weird freaking need we both have to look out for each other?"

Her image in my mind frowned. *You think I'm worried that one of the three most powerful Olympians in the world feels compelled to keep saving my little sister's life?*

"Huh. Well, when you put it that way, it doesn't sound so bad. Except I did it, too. Plus, he's not that powerful right now. He's sick. Like you."

Her expression softened. *You need to ask him about Atlantis. Together, I think you can both do a lot more.*

I nodded. I knew she was right. "Do you think his dragon would see you?

No. Dragons are crazy rare, and crazy dangerous. Hades made it clear you had to be Olympian royalty to see her. And besides, she has no cure.

I nodded again, already knowing that was true. Opening my eyes, I pulled out the little sketchbook. "I'm going to draw the last few days," I told her. "Just in case."

Just in case what?

"I need to see it again."

Good idea, she said, the playful smile back. *Make sure you include that kiss.*

"Lily!"

She shrugged. *It might be important.*

It *was* important. I already knew that. My whole freaking body knew that.

We were both quiet as I made bad pencil sketches in the little book of everything that had happened since I'd arrived back in Aquarius.

When I was done, I stretched, tiredness from the day coursing over me.

"I wonder what the next Trial will be?" I mused aloud as I undressed for bed.

Kryvo's squeaky voice answered. "Hopefully something you can do alongside Poseidon."

"Do you like him?" I asked the starfish, sitting down at the dresser and loosening my tight braid.

"He scares me. But I think he can offer a good alternative to hiding."

I smiled at him. "Good summary. I feel similarly."

I looked at the mirror to check how much of my braid was undone, and my breath caught as my eyes snagged on color.

Not the purple streaks in my hair, but color *on my skin.*

My tattoo was clear on my chest above my bandeau vest, and the very center of the spiral of the shell was blue, the color leaking into turquoise before fading away like a watercolor painting.

"Lily! Lily, my shell!"

The center has color. My sister's voice was tight with what I hoped was excitement.

"Yes! Does this mean I have magic?"

I don't know. I think the whole shell needs color for your power to be present.

"Is something waking it up? Being in Aquarius?"

That is the most likely reason. Or perhaps the magic of the palace is so strong it's waking it up? I don't know.

I scrambled up from the dresser stool and rushed to the window. Looking out at the ocean, I willed myself to feel the pull of the water, that sense of freedom and excitement I had felt on the deck of the ship with Poseidon.

Nothing happened. I just saw masses of blue, raw with power and weight.

"Maybe you're right; the whole thing needs to be filled with color," I conceded.

I'm always right, she answered. I stuck my tongue out as I moved back from the window, excitement still whirring through me.

"Do you think I can speed it up?"

Not without knowing what's caused it, Lily said.

"Good point. Kryvo, can you sense magic?"

"No," answered the starfish. "Poseidon said he can, though."

"He didn't say anything about me having new magic when I saw him earlier." My shoulders slumped a little. "Well, hopefully it keeps filling with color, and then..." And then what? I would be able to do what Lily could? Hold my breath for hours, make water move, swim like I was born of the ocean?

Gods, I hoped so.

I thought my excitement about my tattoo might keep me awake, but my concerns were unfounded. The physicality of the Trial won out over my churning brain, and I slept like the dead.

When I finally roused myself from the peace of sleep, all the thoughts from the previous day crashed back over me. I leaped from the bed to stand in front of the mirror, staring at the tiny splurge of color in the middle of my shell.

"It may be little," I murmured, running my fingers over it, "but it is bright."

And it was. The shade of blue was deep and vivid, and the turquoise ombre a beautiful bright color.

"You slept a long time," squeaked Kryvo. "I was beginning to worry."

"Really?"

"Yes. It is long past midday."

"Huh." I wasn't surprised. I had massively exerted myself the previous day, both physically and mentally.

I made my way into my bathroom, noting that I felt surprisingly good. I expected to have aches and pains from the exertion of being thrown around on the ship, but as I stretched my limbs in the shower, I only felt stronger.

I washed my vest in the large sink, and once it was dry, I dressed in more of the identical clothes from the closet: dark pants and a white shirt over the vest. I couldn't stop staring at the tattoo as I braided my hair.

"Please, please, please let this mean I am a real Nereid."

If my power came to life and my shell colored, maybe that would mean Poseidon would get his heart of the ocean? And then we could heal Lily.

Once I was ready, I realized just how hungry I was. All my mornings in the palace had begun with somebody collecting me from my room, to deliver me to whatever stressful activity was happening next. But today, I had no idea what was coming next.

Putting Kryvo on my collarbone, I cautiously pushed open my bedroom door.

"Holy shit!"

Poseidon was standing in the hall, right outside my room. I clutched the doorframe, my hand on my chest, trying to slow my startled heart rate.

"Are you trying to scare me to death?"

"I was about to knock," he said drily.

I looked at him. He was wearing his fighting garb, and he looked healthy again. No stone was visible on his face. "What do you want?"

He pointed to the wall behind him. The gold paintings of waves were gone, words in their place.

Gather in the ballroom when the sun sets for the second Trial.

I frowned. "Is that from Atlas?"

"Yes."

"How can he make stuff like that happen inside your palace?"

Poseidon scowled. "I don't know. I believe he might have been infiltrating my palace for some time."

"He spoke to me here. In the courtyard," I said.

Fury flashed on Poseidon's face, the smell of the ocean

and the sound of waves crashing over me in a rush. "When?"

"Before the first Trial."

"What did he say?"

"Not a lot. Just wanted to psych me out, I think." I shrugged. "Don't worry about it."

A rumbling sounded in his chest. "Don't worry about it?" he repeated. "My oldest enemy, an ancient, all-powerful Titan is able to roam around my personal palace and intimidate my—" he paused, eyes flicking over me, "*Guests*, and you're telling me not to worry about it?"

"Once you beat him in the Trials, he'll be gone," I said.

Poseidon snarled. "I do not trust the bastard to return my trident, even if I do win."

"Really? Then why compete?"

"For my people." He stood straighter, his jaw clenched. Sweet baby Jesus, he was a fine example of a man.

"Right," I said, trying not to show my thoughts on my face.

"And if I win fairly, my Olympian brethren can back me."

"Of course. Olympian brethren. Known for their fairness." If there was anything most of the Olympian gods were, it was *not* fair. Bored, petty, over-indulged children would be closer to the truth. Poseidon's eyes darkened, but before he could respond to my sarcasm, I stepped out of my room, closing the door behind me. "Where can I get breakfast?"

7

ALMI

"**Y**ou can eat shortly. First, I want to show you something."

He held his hand out, and I took it without question. Last time I had taken his hand he had taken me to the pegasus stables and Blue. If whatever he was showing me this time was even half as good, I wanted in.

To my surprise, he flashed us to the deck of a ship.

I looked around at the shiny planks, gleaming sails, and impressive gold-embellished wheel. "This is a Typhoon," I said, turning in a slow circle.

"I'm impressed," said Poseidon. "You have been studying."

"I have a good memory," I murmured, staring around me as my heart skipped in my chest. "Is this your ship?" *The freaking ship I'd come here for in the first place?*

Poseidon eyed me a moment, then shrugged. "It is one of many ships. But for our purposes, it is an escape plan."

"An escape plan?"

"Atlas is unpredictable, and he hates me. Should anything happen, I want you to come to this ship. It will be here over the palace, at all times, and if you are riding Blue, you will be able to access it."

I stared at him, mouth opening and closing like a goldfish as I tried to pick a question.

"What could happen?" was the question that emerged from my lips first.

"I die."

"You're an immortal god! How the hell would you die?"

"Titans ruled Olympus long before us. And the Olympians only won the war because a few Titans defected and joined us against their own kind."

Fear squished about in my stomach, making me feel a little ill. "He doesn't look as dangerous as you," I said.

Poseidon's chest expanded a little, almost proudly, then his face turned even more serious. "Do not underestimate him. If anything happens to me, you come to this ship on Blue."

"Then what?"

"Then the ship will take you somewhere safe."

"Can you control it if you're..." I didn't want to say dead. My mind was revolting at the idea of Poseidon dying more than it was celebrating the fact that I may have found the ship that could help Lily.

"She'll know what to do." He touched the wood of the railings almost intimately, and I knew then that it was his own ship, not just part of a fleet or something.

"What is she called?"

He looked into my eyes a long moment, and I tried not to squirm. "*Okeánios ánemos.*"

My pulse quickened. It *was* his ship. The only ship that could move underwater as well as through the sky. "She's lovely," I said.

He held my eyes a moment longer, the wildness burning behind that constant stoic control. "There is some color in your shell," he said.

I forgot about the ship completely and looked down at my chest. "Yes! Can you feel if I have any water magic?"

He shook his head. "I can sense no power from you." He held his hands up, clapped, and parted them to reveal two of the vials he had given me before. I took them from him, and as my fingers brushed his palm, that intoxicating sense of freedom powered over me. *My hair whipping around me as I moved fast, no constraints, no rules, no end to the possibilities...*

It wasn't an image so much as a feeling, and it was nothing like anything I had ever felt before coming to the palace.

My whole adult life had been about one singular, all-consuming focus: Lily. The possibility of not having to worry for her life all the time, to be able to just live free...

I wanted it. I wanted it bad.

I realized that Poseidon had tensed, and I was still resting my hand in his, fingers clutching the vials in his palm.

"Oh, sorry," I stuttered, whipping my hand back.

Did he feel something, too?

I risked looking up into his eyes. The froth-tipped waves were crashing in his piercing irises, his jaw clenched tightly. His other hand shot out as mine retracted, and he gripped my shoulder, dropped his head and pulled me toward him. Heat coursed through my body, making my cheeks flush, and a need that was utterly unfamiliar to me pound through my torso, pooling between my legs.

The smell of the ocean surrounded me as I lifted my other hand, unable to stop myself touching his hard, beautiful face. His skin was smooth and hot as I brushed my knuckles down his jaw, and I felt his whole body harden.

"Poseidon," I whispered, as he ducked his head further, his warm breath feathering over my lips as his mouth almost touched mine.

He stopped still.

For a split second, all I could hear was the sound of my own heart trying to pound its way out of my ribcage, then everything flashed white.

I found myself back in front of my bedroom door, and Poseidon stepped back into the corridor, releasing his grip on me. "The ballroom, in a few hours," he barked, and I barely got a glimpse of the wildness in his eyes before he flashed away.

"I don't want to be on you when you and him do that." Kryvo's tiny voice cut through my stunned silence.

"Do what?" I whispered. "What even was that?"

The first kiss I could have put down to adrenaline, or overexcitement. But that? That had come out of nowhere.

No. Not nowhere. If he had felt even a fraction of that blissful feeling I had when our skin had touched, then he could easily have translated that into desire for me.

Is that what I had done? Misread my desperation for a life free of worry as a desperation for him? Maybe I was mixing them up.

Maybe *he* was mixing them up.

I took a deep breath. "Marriage bonds are stupid," I said.

"You seem to quite enjoy it."

I frowned, unable to respond. Did I enjoy it?

Hell yes.

Did I need or understand it?

Fuck no.

I had been on the ship. More than that, Poseidon had told me how to get to it. He had as good as given me a damn key. Blue could take me straight there.

I could go to the stables, get on the pegasus' back, and steal the ship I had come to get that very second.

Except... I couldn't.

Atlas had held me up in front of the whole world of Olympus, and I was as bound to these asshole Trials as much as I was to the king of confusing-emotional-shit, Poseidon.

My ridiculous *husband* had given up his damn trident and realm to save me. I couldn't run. Could I?

"Ohhhh, what a fucking mess." I sagged against the door behind me.

"What's wrong?" Kryvo squeaked.

I hadn't told him about my plan to get the ship and find Atlantis and the legendary healing font. Mostly because I had been suspicious that he was a spy. But that suspicion had leaked away a while back, I realized.

"Let's get some food, and I'll tell you all about it," I said.

8

ALMI

I followed the starfish's directions to a hall that made every other canteen I'd ever seen look, well frankly, shit.

It was a cathedral-like space, with a huge arched ceiling painted with golden waves, and long tables with bench seats lining the hall like pews. All of the tables were covered in food and I walked along them with a plate, loading up with pastries, bread and cold meat cuts.

There were other diners in the room, but not many. I supposed I was too late for the lunch rush. Lots of folk were wearing the blue leather of Poseidon's guard, and I found myself wondering where Galatea was.

"I thought you would die yesterday."

A crisp, clear female voice spoke behind me, and I whirled, nearly dropping my overloaded plate.

Kalypso raised one perfect brow at my food. "That lot might kill you instead," she smiled. Her liquid hair moved around her face, and I tried to shake off my awe. She was regal in her beauty, her rich dark skin glowing with power.

"Did you win?" I asked her. I hadn't thought to ask who came first in the Trial.

She pursed her lips, and her eyes moved from me to somewhere behind me. I glanced over my shoulder but could see nothing.

"No. Ceto won."

"Oh."

Ceto terrified me. Of all the contestants, she was the one I could least imagine ruling a realm. She was a literal monster.

"Oh, indeed. So, how does your husband fare?"

I frowned at her, both at hearing Poseidon described as my husband, but also at her questions. "Good. Why are you talking to me?"

"You are one of us," she said, her eyes a bright icy blue. "One of the five competitors for a place as a ruling god."

Desire burned in her tone, and a true sense of danger started to trickle through me. She wanted the trident and Aquarius. *Bad.*

"Atlas is forcing me to do this. I don't want to rule anything." I decided to seize my opportunity to ask something I'd been wondering about. "Do you have to share Aquarius with him if you win?"

Her features hardened, and my sense of danger heightened. "I share what I want, with who I want," she hissed.

I held my empty hand up in submission. "Okay, I get it. I'm a fan of consent too."

Her eyes narrowed suspiciously, but she relaxed a

little, the power rolling from her lessening a touch. "What are your powers?"

"I'd love to chat, but I have to take this,"—I held up my stacked plate—"to meet a friend."

She stared at me a moment, then shrugged. "Fine. See you at sundown."

"Yeah, see you."

I made my way out of the dining hall as quickly as I could. I hadn't intended to take my food back to my room, and I certainly wasn't going to tell her that the friend I was meeting was a tiny magic starfish, but I didn't want to spend any more time with Kalypso than I had to. Being in her company felt like being with a ticking timebomb, a weird pressure pushing at my mind the whole time her eyes were on me.

Maybe that was a god thing. I shook my head as I hurried along the corridors.

"You missed a turn," squeaked Kryvo.

"Good thing I've got you with me," I muttered to him, backing up.

Eventually I found my room and I wolfed down everything I'd put on my plate, using my dresser as a table. As I ate, I told Kryvo what I had read in the book and about the Font of Zoi.

"So, I'm thinking that if I can get to the font, then I can cure Lily of both the sleeping sickness and the stone blight," I finished, stuffing the last of a small meat pie into my mouth.

"There are a few problems with your plan," said Kryvo, his little suckers squelching on the dresser surface.

"Just a few?" I muttered.

"Firstly, and most importantly, if Poseidon knows about this font, he would have visited it and used it himself already."

I nodded slowly. "Yes. I know, I... I have to ask him about it, I guess."

"You do not want to?"

"I don't want him to say it won't work," I said, realizing the truth of the words as I said them. "Atlantis is my only hope. If Poseidon tells me it won't work, then I have nothing."

"That's not true. Poseidon said that the Oracle told him the stone blight can be cured by the heart of the ocean, correct?"

"Yes."

"If your power awakens then you might make the prophecy possible."

"Maybe." I looked at the starfish. "I don't think pinning my hopes on my absent magic is a very solid plan though."

"I don't like to upset you, Almi, but if the Oracle said that the heart of the ocean is the only way to cure the blight then..."

"Then my font won't work," I said on a sigh.

"It looks that way. I think you should reset your focus on finding out more about this heart."

I stared at him, not really seeing anything. My glum acknowledgment of his words was working its way through me, and I was trying to keep my anger at bay. It wasn't fair that this had happened to Lily. She was a good person and had been her whole life. Selfless and kind. Why should she, and all the other families in Aquarius, be affected by this blight? *Poseidon included.*

I didn't have the emotional capacity to work out why I felt a surge of panic when I thought about him turning to stone again and was relieved when Kryvo spoke. "Do you want me to see if there is anything in the palace about the heart of the ocean?"

"Could you? That's a great idea."

The starfish wiggled his arms. "Of course. I am your friend."

I smiled at him. "Yes. You are. Thank you."

He was right. I should move my focus to finding out about the heart. If Poseidon and the Oracle were right, then Lily and I were connected to it somehow. And I couldn't steal the damn ship and get to Atlantis anyway, not while I was bound to the Trials. I needed to set aside the certainty I felt that there were answers there and concentrate on the heart of the ocean.

A knock on my door a short while later turned out to be the two nymphs who had dressed me for the start of the Trials.

"Hello. Please come with us to the dressing rooms to be prepared," the small one said.

I followed them dutifully, taking Kryvo with me. He didn't camouflage himself, and both nymphs kept giving him small, disapproving glances.

"You've decided not to hide anymore?" I asked him.

"Poseidon knows I am here, and they all saw you talking to me in the Trials. If you insist on me accompanying you, then I may as well save my energy."

I was sure I heard a hint of pride in his voice. Maybe my cowardly little starfish was getting a teensy bit braver.

"Good. Be proud, Kryvo," I told him.

We reached the dressing rooms and I looked at the nymph next to me. "This is my friend, and I'm going to need an outfit that he looks good with." I was joking, but I felt Kryvo warm a little. The nymph raised their eyebrows, then raised a hand to their chin thoughtfully.

"We can make that work."

9

ALMI

Somewhat to my surprise, the nymphs dressed me perfectly to match Kryvo. They put me in a corset dress, the top half the same shape as my vest, leaving everything above my breasts and my shoulders completely bare. At first, I felt uncomfortable with so much skin on show, but when I swished around in front of the mirror, the full bottom of the dress weighing nothing and moving like liquid, I decided I liked it. The dress was jet-black, a color I hadn't expected to suit me. But with my bright red starfish accessory, it looked good. And there was another splash of color showing in the mirror.

"Can you see the tattoo on my chest?" I asked the nymph.

"Yes. It was not there last time."

"Huh."

Poseidon must have lifted the glamor hiding it. The vivid blue and turquoise center caught my eye, the black gown only enhancing it.

The nymphs put my hair up in an elaborate knot, much of it curled and falling in tendrils that looked effortless, but that they had actually carefully arranged. More streaks of blue had joined the purple, I noticed.

My makeup was done the same as it had been last time, subtly, but making me look older in a way that I liked.

"You guys are really good at this," I said when they were finished.

They both nodded. "Yes."

I smiled. "Thanks."

With more nods, they bowed their heads and left the room, just as Galatea appeared in the doorway.

"Hi," I said.

"Good evening."

"You coming to the ballroom too?"

"Yes. Why is there a starfish on you? Is that jewelry?"

"He's my emotional support starfish."

Galatea just shook her head and held the door open for me. I heard her muttering the word odd as I walked past her.

"Any ideas what the next Trial will be about?" I asked her.

"No. But Poseidon told me he has shown you the *Okeánios ánemos.*"

"Yes."

"Good. I will meet you aboard if anything happens."

"Would you not have to take Poseidon's place if anything happens to him?"

Her pace slowed as she threw a surprised look at me. "No. Aquarius must be ruled by a god."

"What are you?"

She paused before answering me, her pace quickening along the corridors again. "A nymph".

"You must be a very powerful nymph, to be Poseidon's General."

"Yes," was all she said.

Sensing her reluctance to talk about it anymore, I changed the subject. "Kalypso spoke to me earlier. She wants to win."

Galatea pulled a face. "I've no doubt. She is the strongest in the competition. Apart from the king, of course."

If Poseidon was at full strength that might have been true, but I refrained from correcting her. "Ceto scares me," I said instead.

"Ceto has been under Poseidon's control for all of time. This will be a hard rift to heal, once the Trials are over."

"Was she under his control voluntarily?"

"It was a mutual arrangement. Poseidon let her and her brother create all manner of hellish creatures, in return for allegiance. For the most part, they had free run of the deep. He was not abusing his position," she said, with a severe look.

"I wasn't suggesting that he was. Just trying to under-stand how she might see it."

"She has betrayed his allegiance. There is no more to it than that."

Galatea's unending loyalty to her king was admirable, but I wasn't surprised it wasn't echoed by Ceto. In fact, there were likely a number of Poseidon's subjects who resented being controlled by a god their whole lives, especially if like Ceto, they had so much power of their own. "I heard she won the last Trial," I said.

"Yes. She has the most shells now. But that will change," Galatea replied fiercely.

We reached the large, familiar double doors to the ballroom, and she pushed them open.

The room looked the same as the last time I'd been there, except there was now a large chair in the middle of the room. It was made from hundreds of interlocking rings that made up globes, and there was no question it was representative of Atlas' sigil.

Atlas himself was lounging in the throne, the light from the beautiful coral reef surrounding the ballroom playing across his face as his eyes found mine. A cruel smile twisted the corners of his mouth.

Galatea growled low in her throat. "That bastard sits on a throne in the true King's own palace?"

I looked around for Poseidon, and found him instantly. He was standing with Hades, the two of them talking quietly. He was wearing the ocean robe, waves washing over the fabric and drawing everyone who passed him's gaze.

I scanned the rest of the room quickly, noting that the audience was mostly the same as last time, the same Olympian gods—and the same three missing.

I started to move toward Poseidon, but before I took one step, Atlas rose.

"You're here, *Queen* Almi!"

I stalled in both movement and thought.

Queen.

Well, that was new.

I glanced at Poseidon, but his angry eyes were fixed on Atlas.

"We have been awaiting your arrival so that we may begin the festivities. And may I say how lovely you look?"

I gave him a sarcastic smile, then flipped him the finger.

My knees buckled beneath me, and I cried out in shock as my body folded itself over into a groveling bow.

"Atlas!" roared Poseidon's voice, and the compulsion controlling my body vanished.

"She must learn to respect those more powerful than her, Poseidon," Atlas said, voice silky sweet. "Which, I believe, is everybody."

Fury coursed through my veins as I got to my feet. "Prick," I hissed through my teeth. I knew he heard me, because his eyes narrowed, and a fizz of pain jolted through my body. It was gone before I could suck in a breath, though, and he turned back to the rest of the room.

"Citizens of Olympus, honored Olympians," he called, spreading his arms wide. "Welcome. As it stands, Ceto has four shells, Kalypso three, Polybotes two, Almi one, and Poseidon,"—he turned to the sea god. "None."

Thunder cracked in the distance, and the coral reef's bright pastel glow flickered dark for a split second.

I had more shells than Poseidon? Shit. That must be because it was my ship that had flown over the finish-line. His had never made it.

"The next three Trials will be a feast for your senses, good people!"

He clapped his hands and a massive flame dish appeared in place of his throne. Flames leaped high in it, flashed a white-hot color, then an image appeared in them.

"Apollo has graciously agreed to host the first of three elemental themed Trials. As his realm has the most extreme temperatures, it seemed fitting to hold the ice Trial there."

The image of a cliff made from solid ice moved as though a drone was panning, and I felt my muscles tense as I saw something huge and dark moving inside the ice. The image swooped to show a sheet of ice that seemed to go on forever at the foot of the cliff, with more dark shapes moving beneath it in the sea below.

Atlas' eyes glinted with cruel excitement as he spoke. "You must collect as many shells as you can in one hour. But be warned, the only way to leave the Trial is to find the red shell. Without it, you cannot return."

Fear gripped my gut, and I felt hot at just the thought of being trapped.

"The second of the elements will be earth, hosted in Aphrodite's deadly tropical seagardens."

The image changed to a panning view of a series of tropical islands. As the view swooped closer to the water, I could see green beneath the surface, then red liquid began to seep like blood through the water, obliterating the green below.

"The last will be fire, held where the volcanoes of Hephaestus' Scorpio meet the depths of Aquarius."

Once more, the image changed, this time to a scene below the surface of the water. Everything was dark and gloomy, except for a searing river of molten lava carving its way through jagged black rock.

"Do we take it in turns or all do it together?" Polybotes' deep voice rumbled from where he stood on the other side of the room, towering over everyone else.

"No. You will decide what order you take on the Trials, now."

My heart was beating too quickly as I looked at Poseidon. His eyes met mine, and I knew we were thinking the same thing. If we were going to work together, we had to choose the same order as each other.

10

ALMI

I began to move toward Poseidon, but after one step, my feet froze. I tried to pick them up off the ground, but they wouldn't obey me. More anger surged through me as I looked at Atlas.

"You will be choosing in private," he smiled.

"Choose the—" Poseidon's voice in my head was abruptly cut off.

"There will be no mental communication, either." Atlas looked at Poseidon, and I thought for a minute the sea god would throw himself at the smug Titan.

Hades laid a hand on Poseidon's shoulder, and he flinched.

Atlas gave a small chuckle. "Ceto, as the leader, you will choose first." He clapped his hands again and the flame dish vanished, replaced by a table with three small, identical urns on it.

"He shouldn't have this much power in the palace," hissed Galatea quietly. "I will find out how he is doing this if it kills me."

"Can you speak to Poseidon in your head?" I whispered to her.

She concentrated a moment, then shook her head. "No."

"Shit."

Ceto emerged from the crowd, and she slithered on her many creepy, rotten looking octopus legs up to the table. Silently, she leaned over the urns, then moved two of them so that they were in a different order. I watched carefully, but I could see no indication that there was anything on them that determined which was which, or even that they were different from each other.

"Kalypso?" Atlas said when Ceto moved back from the table.

The beautiful Titan was wearing scarlet red and looked as fierce as a lion as she stepped forward. As fierce as a loin-fish, I corrected myself mentally as she made her way to the table, her water-hair swishing. She reordered all of the urns before stepping back with a nod.

My stomach felt uncomfortably jumpy as I watched Polybotes stomp over next.

Poseidon's plan for us to stick together had clearly been anticipated by Atlas.

I looked at the Titan I had been repeatedly told not to underestimate. He looked like a man. A normal, if a little hotter than usual, middle-aged human. Tanned skin, symmetrical, good-looking face, and the build of someone who went to the gym a lot.

Sensing me looking, he fixed his dark eyes on mine. I swallowed, about to look away, when his whole appearance changed. It was only for a split second, but for that second, he was made of freaking fire. Everything other than his eyes were flame-red, sparks of deadly power running in rivers across his whole body. Those eyes, though… Black pits of nothingness, a promise of an eternity of soulless, lifeless *nothing*.

His human image flashed back into place, a cold smile on his handsome face, and gooseflesh erupted over my skin.

"Can he read my mind?" I asked Galatea out of the side of my mouth. It was too much of a coincidence that I had been thinking about his appearance for him to give me a flash of himself looking so terrifying.

"The palace forbids mind-reading as part of its magic, but Atlas has been thwarting its magic since he got here, so fuck knows."

It was the first time I'd heard her swear, and I turned a little to her. Her sternness had amplified tenfold, and I felt a bolt of sympathy for her. She loved Poseidon and Aquarius; that much was clear. And that meant everything she loved was under very serious threat. Hatred for Atlas oozed from her every pore.

"Can I stop it?"

She glanced at me. "Not with no magic. But I can try to shield your thoughts."

"You can do that?"

"I can try. Take my staff."

"Thank you," I said, as she passed me her staff as subtly as possible.

Polybotes had finished rearranging the urns, and Atlas looked at me.

"Almi's turn," he said, gesturing at the table.

I strode up, keeping the staff by my side and gripping it hard. I had a plan, but I had no idea if I could pull it off.

When I reached the urns, they all flared to life with a deep red glow, and writing in a messy scrawl burned in the ceramic: Fire, Ice, Earth. One label on each urn.

Shrugging, I put them in the order Atlas had introduced them, in the hope that Poseidon might instinctively do the same if my plan failed.

I moved the pot that read ice to the left, put the earth one in the middle, and the fire one last.

When I turned away from the table, just as I had hoped, Poseidon was waiting a few feet behind me.

"Kryvo," I said as quietly as I could, without moving my lips. "Tell Poseidon what order I put the urns in." As swiftly as I could, I moved my hand to my collar and lifted the starfish from my skin as I walked toward Poseidon, my back to Atlas.

Poseidon's eyebrows rose as I walked straight at him, holding his gaze and trying to send my best 'just-go-with-it' vibes.

"Good luck, husband," I said loudly, and pressed my lips to his in the most over-the-top manner I could, whilst also pressing Kryvo to the shoulder his toga left exposed. The starfish gave a tiny, startled squeak, and it felt like Poseidon had turned to stone again, he was so still. He flared to life suddenly, gripping my waist and pulling me into him, his lips moving beneath mine. Heat rushed me, my stomach swooping, and I heard Atlas bark.

"Enough of this nonsense. Poseidon, choose your urns."

Poseidon stepped back, and I dragged my eyes from

his to glance at his shoulder. Kryvo had camouflaged himself completely.

I walked slowly back to Galatea. "I think it worked," I whispered to her. Atlas had said nothing, and Poseidon was moving the urns with a sense of purpose.

"What did you do? Where is your ornamental starfish?"

"Hopefully saving my ass. Again."

Poseidon moved back from the table, and Atlas waved his hands. The table vanished and the throne reappeared as he began to read the order the first three competitors had chosen. I barely heard what he said until he said my name. My pulse quickened and I fixed my eyes on Poseidon. He stared straight back at me.

It was him who had suggested us working together, but now it seemed I had been keener on the idea than I had realized. More than anything in the world, I wanted the moody ocean god by my side when we faced the Trials we had just been given a glimpse of.

"Almi chose Ice, then Earth, then Fire."

I knew instantly that my plan had worked. I saw the flicker of light in Poseidon's eyes, and the coral reef around us pulsed with the faintest glimmer of energy.

Atlas' voice was hard when he spoke again. "Poseidon is taking on Ice, then Earth, then Fire, too."

Galatea gripped my arm. "That means you'll be in the Ice level with the giant, the Earth level with Kalypso, and the Fire level with Ceto. You need to be on your guard," she said, face tight with concern. She'd obviously been listening more carefully than I had.

"I will. And I'll be with Poseidon, thanks to you

shielding my thoughts and one tiny starfish." I grinned, holding her staff out.

She took it, a slightly puzzled frown on her face. "I'm glad I could help."

"I've had an idea!" Atlas' voice boomed across the room, loud enough that it made my pain lance through my skull. We turned to him, and I was alarmed to see that his placid, smug expression had been replaced with something bordering on manic.

"I think we should start now."

"What?" Kalypso's voice was crisp and clear in the stunned silence. "No, we need time to prepare."

"No, I don't think you do." Atlas' unhinged glare was trained on Poseidon. "Let's do this now. Off you go!"

The world flashed white, and the next thing I knew, I was underwater.

11

ALMI

My immediate instinct was to draw breath, and I barely stopped myself in time. Panic swamped me as I began to sink through the water, and I kicked my legs, trying to orientate myself.

I didn't have my belt. I had no water-root.

The overwhelming sense of being trapped pressed in on me, the weight of the water crushing me on every side. Something moved around me, freezing cold currents blasting my body, and then Poseidon's face was in front of me, his bright blue eyes beacons in the gloom. He gripped my face with his hands, then drew my lips to his.

Air, I realized dimly, as his mouth closed over mine.

He was giving me air.

He pulled away from me, eyes boring into mine. The burn in my lungs lessened and I tried to concentrate.

Where the fuck were those bubbles that had helped me last time?

The skirt of my dress tangled in my legs, and I stopped

kicking. Poseidon was holding me still in the water, and I needed to conserve my energy.

Bright red pulsed lower on Poseidon's body, and I realized it was Kryvo. Reaching out, I pulled him gently from Poseidon skin and placed him on my bare collarbone. The water was freezing, and he felt warm against my skin.

"Make those bubbles come back!" the little starfish squeaked as soon as his little stingers had latched on.

I shook my head, unable to answer him. I looked into Poseidon's eyes, wondering if he could speak to me.

His mouth moved, his words carrying to me through the water and sounding as though they were very far away. "We need to find a way of you breathing."

No shit.

I saw movement over his shoulder in the water, along with flashes of red. Fear made my skin feel icy cold as it got closer, and I realized what it was.

"Rotblood!" squeaked Kryvo. I gripped Poseidon's arm and pointed frantically over his shoulder.

He turned just in time, raising one of his fists. Water pulsed out from him, swirling in a glowing blue current as it powered toward the rotten, red shark. The current wrapped itself around the creature, and then the thing exploded.

Poseidon turned back to me, drawing me close and breathing air into my shaking body again. "We will not be able to keep this up for long," he said, the words slow and hard to decipher. A granite tendril worked its way across the side of his jaw.

Where were those damned bubbles? Who had sent

them last time? I hadn't even thought to ask Persephone or Galatea if they had helped, though I couldn't think of anyone else who would want to assist me.

Whoever you are, please, please, please help me again now, I prayed. If we didn't find the red shell, we would be trapped in here forever. Which in my case, wouldn't be very long, given that I was mortal and we were submerged in freezing, shark-infested water.

Something lifted my hair from my face. Something that wasn't Poseidon. A stream of tiny bubbles whizzed around me, faster and faster, until it settled around my face, just as it had done before.

Poseidon's eyebrows raised, and I took a tiny, experimental breath.

Air. Cool dry air.

"The bubbles are back!" I exclaimed aloud.

"You can breathe?"

"Yes."

"Tell me how later. Now, we need to find shells." Poseidon's gurgled voice was clipped and to the point, as though he was conserving words. "I can't afford to lose this Trial."

His face was as serious as I had ever seen it, the water lifting his white hair behind him, his tense body like a coiled spring. The importance of what he was saying settled over me.

When it had just been me, the aim of the game was just to survive. But now we were working together, the stakes had changed. We had to make sure Poseidon got his realm and his trident back. That meant actually doing well.

Winning.

I nodded, and he took my hand.

He moved through the water like a dart, pulling me along by his side. I didn't need to kick my legs or move my arms at all, so I just clung on tightly and kept my eyes open for anything that looked like a shell.

As we sped through the water, I assumed that we were under the sheet of ice that had been in the image in the flame dish, but all I could see was the dusky gloom of blue water, so filled with tiny particles that it was hard to see far. Below us was inky darkness, and no sound carried to my ears.

I hoped Poseidon had an idea where we were going, because I had none whatsoever.

"Look for shells," I told Kryvo, trying to distract myself from the cold by talking to the little starfish. The bubbles were still whizzing around my head, keeping a layer of air between my face and the water. My voice sounded completely normal to me, and Kryvo's little voice came back to me clearly.

"Not if they are anywhere near rotbloods," he shuddered.

"You did great, telling Poseidon what order to put the urns in," I told him, trying to cheer him up.

"I do not want to be stuck to him again," he said seriously.

"No?"

"No. He is… intense."

I inadvertently gripped the god's hand harder as we sped along through the water.

Intense was the word.

12

ALMI

After a minute or two, when I was fairly sure I couldn't feel my feet—which were fortunately encased in sandals that laced halfway up my calf and therefore still on—I saw something. A solid wall of bright blue ice.

Almost the same color as Poseidon's eyes, the vertical expanse was like glass. My heart gave a little stutter when Poseidon pulled us closer.

There, encased in the ice wall but moving jerkily, as though trapped in mud, was the creature that had attacked him at the end of the last Trial. The beast that looked like it should have been in a nightmare version of Jurassic Park.

"What is that thing?"

It moved again inside the ice, easily twenty times my size, as we hovered the other side of the endless wall.

It was on its back, curved like a half-moon, arms and claws reaching up, scraping and twitching at its icy prison. One reptilian eye locked onto Poseidon and its massive mouth opened in obvious anger. A cracking noise sounded in the distance, and fear lurched through me.

"We should go. Now."

"It can't escape the ice," Poseidon's gurgled, slow reply came.

It moved again, its maw snapping closed, and one of its six brutally sharp arms jerking a few inches.

"All the same. Lots of shells, one hour to find them. We should leave him alone." My teeth were chattering as I spoke.

Poseidon glanced at me, then began to move, pulling me along with him.

I estimated it was another five minutes of swimming along the mammoth ice wall before a beam of light cut through the water like a laser before us.

Poseidon angled up toward it immediately, and relief rushed me as I saw a bright circle of light above us. As we swam higher, the water around us lightened, and I could see the layer of ice over our heads clearly. And the small, perfectly round hole in it.

Suspicion made me slow, pulling Poseidon's hand. "What if it's a trap? Surely shells should be under the water?"

He frowned at me. "Do you see any shells under here?"

He gestured at the empty expanse, the only thing catching my eye the moving silhouette of the monster trapped in the ice wall.

I shook my head. Slowly, he let go of my hand. My fingers were so numb with cold he had to uncurl them himself.

He swam to the hole, and anxiety gripped me as he

slowly moved his head up through it. His arms followed, and he heaved himself out of the water. I watched his legs disappear up and out, then looked for his shadow through the ice.

I could see nothing.

I kicked my legs and moved my arms in a wide arc, swimming closer to the hole, heart pounding.

Movement made me cry out in tense surprise, until I realized it was his arm plunging back into the water, his fingers extended.

Without hesitating, I reached out and grabbed his hand, letting him pull me out of the water.

The freezing air washed over my skin painfully as he yanked me up onto the ice. I stumbled, my numb feet not working properly, and wrapped my arms around my exposed chest. My sopping wet skirt clung to my legs as I looked around.

Well, it was marginally better than the emptiness under the ice, but not by much.

The ice wall we had been swimming along extended high above the water, forming the cliff that we had seen in the flame dish image. At its base, where the ice met the wall, was something that looked, from a distance, like it was made of metal. Something man- or god-made.

"D-d-d-d-o we n-n-n-eed t-t-to go over there?" I stuttered, pointing.

Poseidon scowled at me. "If we stayed in the water any longer you would have died from the cold."

"Th-th-that's hardly my fault," I protested. "I d-d-didn't ask to come out here in a fucking b-b-ballgown."

Baring his teeth, he undid the belt at his waist, sliding his ocean toga from his body.

I tried to keep my frozen face still, but I could feel my eyebrows raising.

When he'd completely removed the toga, I found myself staring at him in nothing but a small, relatively tight pair of black shorts, and one gold strap holding a dagger and some sort of flute across his shoulder that had been previously covered. A black leather thong was around his neck, a small blue gem on it hanging between his sculpted pecs.

I blinked at him. "You took your c-c-clothes off," I said thickly.

"I don't feel the cold." He held out his toga. "Take it," he barked, when I continued to stare at him.

I did, and his hand glowed around the fabric before he let go. "It will keep you warm. Put it on now, we have wasted enough time."

"I don't know how to wear a toga," I said, shaking out the huge piece of fabric. It looked like waves were rolling over it, shining with metallic threads as they crashed. It was beautiful.

"I don't give a shit how you wear it, just don't die of hypothermia!" He stamped his foot, jolting me into action.

"Right, got it, don't d-d-die," I said, wrapping the toga around myself like a blanket. Warmth enveloped me immediately, making me realize just how much my body was seizing up.

With one last glare, Poseidon turned and began striding across the ice toward the metal thing in the distance.

"Are you not worried about the ice breaking?" I called as I hurried after him.

He didn't reply, so I took that as a no.

I was, though, and took care to make sure that everywhere I put my feet looked solid before I stepped. It would be just my luck to fall through the ice straight into the waiting jaws of a frigging rotblood. And I knew there were more under there. Every now and then I saw a flash of something dark and red in the depths.

But then I caught a flash of something else in the ice, as I carefully avoided the area around another perfectly round hole.

Something shining like mother-of-pearl, catching the pale white light.

"Poseidon, wait!" I dropped to my knees, peering closely.

There, embedded in the ice, was a shell. Not a red shell that would get us out of here, but a shell nonetheless.

Poseidon appeared beside me, and I was momentarily distracted by the sheer amount of tanned flesh in my immediate vicinity, before he spoke.

"How do we get it out of the ice?"

"Your dagger?" I gestured at the little weapon on his strap. "Good thing one of us attended a ball armed."

"I am always armed," he said seriously.

I didn't doubt it.

He took the dagger in his right hand and pressed the tip to the ice. A loud cracking sounded, and I scooted backward on my knees.

"I'm going to wait just over here," I said.

"Good idea," he answered, without looking at me.

He began to dig the shell out of the ice, and thin cracks snaked out from where he worked. I kept moving toward the cliff and the metal structure as the cracks spread, but I was reluctant to get too far from him.

"The cracks are getting pretty big now," I called to him, at least ten feet away now.

I heard a small thudding noise, and Kyrvo squeaked in alarm as I looked down.

I was on ice thin enough to see through, straight down into the unblinking, onyx eyes of a rotblood. More rotten red shapes moved beneath the ice and as I looked out at Poseidon, I realized they were gathering under him too.

Making just one of the monsters explode had caused a reaction from the stone to show on his face. How many rotbloods would he be able to handle before he exerted too much power and turned into a statue again?

"Poseidon?" I started to shout, but he cut me off.

He didn't look up. He spoke one word, clearly and loudly. "Run."

13

ALMI

He stood up and cracking sounded so loudly I gasped. My legs moved instinctively, and before I knew it, I was sprinting full pelt toward the cliff, and what I desperately hoped was land.

Throwing a glance over my shoulder, I saw Poseidon running behind me, catching me up. Around him, the ice was breaking apart, the red-and-black, lava-like snouts of the demon sharks snapping at his feet as they tried to propel themselves up out of the water.

Why wasn't he flashing to safety? Surely gods didn't run!

"Faster!" he roared, and I turned back, urging more strength into my legs.

The ice under my feet heaved, and a small shriek escaped my lips as I dove to the side, leaping for another piece of ice as the one I had been racing across tilted into the water below. Red and black flashed in my peripheral vision, but I didn't stop to look.

Throwing myself at what I could now see was a metal platform, was the only thing in my mind. I caught the freezing cold railing of the platform and pulled myself onto it, the heavy material of my dress wrapping around my legs as I skidded, Poseidon's toga falling to the metal. Half a second later Poseidon's bare feet slammed onto the platform and he slowed to a stop, whirling back. The chunks of ice that had once been the perfect sheet covering the sea were sinking into the water, the rotbloods snapping at them.

"Christ on a cracker," I panted. "That was close."

Poseidon turned back to me, holding out the small white shell. "Do you have somewhere safe to store this?"

I glanced inadvertently down at his underwear, the only thing he was wearing, then nodded. He passed me the shell, and I tucked it into the tight bra I wore under the corset dress. He watched me, eyes flaring with light.

"Wear the toga," he growled, as I met his gaze. Nodding, I picked it up from where it had fallen, wrapping it around my shoulders. "We need to keep moving."

I turned away from the shark-infested water to inspect my surroundings. The ice cliff rose on our left, its surface like glass and the dark shape of the epic beast inside it no longer visible. The platform shuddered, and I peered over the edge to see the sharks biting at the metal posts it was standing on.

The other end of the platform, to my relief, was attached to land. Ice and snow-covered land, but land all the same.

I made my way across the metal, keen to get away from the sharks. "Don't they find it cold in there? They look like they're made of lava," I said. "Ice and lava don't seem to go together."

"They can survive in any environment. They are born of lava, but they are made of blood and rotten flesh."

I swallowed back my nausea.

"Hence the name," I mumbled. "What's the thing in the ice called?"

"A talontaur. And it's a she."

"Is it related to the one you killed before you turned to stone?"

Poseidon glanced at me, then shook his head. "It is the same one."

"How is that possible?"

"Demons and monsters of Olympus do not die. They regenerate. She will be trapped in there until she is at full power, and a god releases her."

"A god like you?"

"Or Ceto. But without my trident, I can't control her. Come."

Snow crunched under his feet as he began walking along the frozen ground.

"Your toes are going to fall off," I told him, walking after him and trying not to watch the way the muscles in his back moved as he strode along.

He ignored me.

"I am glad to be out of the water," Kryvo squeaked.

"You and me both," I told him. "But I don't know where we'll find shells out here."

We were on a shore of some description, but it was far

from the sandy beach on Sagittarius that had housed the treasure chest puzzle.

The smell in the air was of pine and frost, and the sound of the ocean was distinct in its absence, after being around it for so many days now.

I strained my ears, listening for anything at all, but only the odd cracking from the frozen sea behind us was audible, save for our footsteps.

We were hugging the ice wall, moving farther inland, toward a large copse of snow-covered trees. Nothing seemed to be on the ground, other than a few scrubby plants and boulders. I inspected everything we walked past carefully, just in case.

"Do you know where you're going?" I asked Poseidon, as he angled toward the trees.

"No."

"Then how do you know all the shells aren't under the water, and there's nothing up here?"

"Atlas wants me to lose. I am a water god. You are a sea nymph. He will make it hard for us by making the challenge one of dry land."

I frowned as I considered his words. "But Ceto and Kalypso are sea gods too."

"Neither are as powerful as me," he growled.

I opened my mouth to comment on the stone affliction, but remembered everything was being broadcast. Unsure whether to bring it up or not, I bit my lip.

"What-" I started, but Poseidon froze, holding up his hand.

"Listen," he whispered.

I did, catching the faint sound of a man shouting, then a screeching. "Polybotes?" I whispered.

"Maybe." He started up again, moving in the direction of the sound.

"How long do you think we have left?" I asked him.

"About half an hour," he replied quietly.

"Twenty-eight minutes," Kryvo squeaked. "I checked a palace clock when we started."

"Clever starfish," I told him, and he heated briefly on my skin.

We continued toward the copse of trees, and the light got darker as we moved away from the ice cliff. I guessed it was reflecting so much light that anything would feel dark in comparison.

The ground was still bare, just glistening frost-covered boulders and a smattering of snow. When we reached the first tree though, I paused.

They were conifers, the long thin branches covered in very dark green needles, which were, in turn, covered in snow. But something about them wasn't right.

Poseidon had moved farther into the copse, and I called his name softly.

"The trees," he answered. "There's something about them."

I turned to him as he took one branch at its base and shook. Powdery snow fell in a shower to the ground, and Poseidon shook the branch again. Slowly, the pine needles began to change color. In a few seconds, the whole branch, and then the whole tree, was yellow.

"What the...?"

"Try that one," Poseidon said, and I reached out and

did the same to the branch in front of me. The snow fell first, and then the tree turned blue.

I couldn't help the grin that sprang to my lips. "This is cool."

Light flared in Poseidon's eyes, then they narrowed. "Check all the trees. We need one shell-colored."

"White?"

"Or red."

Excitement buzzed through me as we began to move through the little copse of pines, shaking every branch we could reach. Eventually, all the snow fell from the one I was gripping and when the green pine-needles began to change color, it was to the exact same shade of white as the snow that had dropped to the ground.

"I have a white one!" I called.

"I have a red one," Poseidon's voice answered. He sounded alarmingly far away, but I didn't have time to worry about it, because the tree started to rumble.

The branches vibrated, and I took a step back, unsure what to do. "Any ideas, Kryvo?" I started to ask, when snow blasted up out of the ground in a circle around the trunk of the tree.

I took another stumbling step back, but I was too slow, and snow churned up around my feet, lifting my skirts and the toga away from me. I clung on, whirling, trying to move clear of the sudden snowstorm. Every time I tried to step out of the circle, I was blasted back. The only place I could see that was clear was underneath the low branches of the pine tree, so I ducked to my knees and began to crawl under.

The snow rose higher, whipping my wet hair around

my face and filling my nose and mouth as I crawled. I coughed, wiping uselessly at my face with one hand as I clung desperately to the toga with my other.

With a rush, a current of air flowed around me, warm and nothing like the stinging snow-filled air of the storm. Just like the bubbles, it swirled around my face, creating a barrier between me and the choking snow.

I took a gratefully deep breath, then forced my way under the tree. The needles scratched my bare shoulders as I tucked myself in, gripping the rough bark.

Concern for Poseidon rose in me, but I doubted snow would choke him. Snow was made of water, after all. I waited for what felt like an age, but was probably only a few minutes, until the snow died down and eventually stopped. Cautiously, I crawled out of the small space.

"Almi?" Poseidon's voice reached me, and then he was there, pulling me to my feet. The warm current of air had vanished, and I blinked up at him. His hair was wild and windswept.

"I hid from the snow under the tree," I said, and his eyes flickered to my hair. He reached out and pulled a white pine-needle from the strands.

"There are a few more," he said. His voice held a gentle quality that I had only heard him use when talking about his subjects before.

"I'll get them later. Did you get the red shell?"

He shook his head. "No. But the storm revealed a path. Did you get the white shell?"

I shook my head, turning back to the tree. As the only white one in what was now a sea of orange, blue, green, yellow and purple trees, it stood out.

"You know, you should make a forest like this in Aquarius, of multi-colored trees," I told him. "I would, if I was a god."

He looked at me a moment, shook his head, then looked back to the white tree. I scanned it too, looking for a shell, or a path.

"There." I followed Poseidon's pointing arm to the very tip of the tree. A shining mother-of-pearl nautilus shell perched up there like a frigging Christmas tree star.

Poseidon held out his hand, and it glowed a brief second before snow lifted from the ground in a flurry. It whipped quickly into a ribbon of water, melting fast, then flicked up to the top of the tree. When it whizzed back down again, it deposited the shell in Poseidon's waiting hand, then dripped lifeless back to the frozen ground.

I tried not to be impressed, but the simple act made me covet his powers more than watching him make rotten sharks explode.

It reminded me of the things Lily used to do with water, I realized with a pang of sadness.

For the first time since starting the Trial, her image flared to life in my mind.

You're doing great, she said.

I nodded, then held out my hand. Poseidon dropped the shell into it, then very deliberately turned away as I tucked it into my bra.

"Let's get this red shell," I said, to let him know I was done. He strode off through the vividly colored forest without turning back, and I rolled my eyes as I hurried after him.

14

ALMI

"You know, you're not very polite," I said to his annoyingly pleasing bare shoulders.

"Nor are you."

I bristled at his response. "I'm very polite. Maybe not to you, but in general, I don't wander off when people are talking, and I look at them when they speak to me."

He glanced over his shoulder at me, a tiny sparkle of something that wasn't anger in his eyes.

I needed a frigging book to decipher his emotions. They were literally unrecognizable, he controlled them so well.

He pointed as we reached a tree with scarlet-colored pine-needles, and a very deliberate trail of the little red needles leading away from it, out of the copse.

"Looks suspicious," I said.

"We only have about fifteen minutes left. We need the red shell to leave this place, and I can't flash." Tension laced his words.

"How can Atlas remove your flashing and your talking-in-my-head thing?"

"When we agree to compete in Trials, we agree to the rules of the Trials," he ground out. "Now that he controls the Trials, he controls us."

I pulled a face, then looked up at the sky through the trees. "Atlas, if you're watching, you're a massive jerk," I yelled.

When I looked back down, Poseidon was shaking his head. "You are like a child," he said.

"Well, you're like an old man." *A really frigging hot old man.* "You should try acting like a child sometime. You might enjoy being a bit less serious."

"Whilst risking our lives in a deadly timed Trial, you're suggesting I goad the ancient Titan who put us here?" Anger was creeping into his words.

"Yes."

He stared at me a beat longer, then to my surprise tilted his head back and roared at the sky.

"Atlas, you are a weak-minded gràson."

"Feel better?" I asked him when he looked back down.

"Not really. We need to go."

He turned to follow the trail of red needles.

"What does gràson mean?"

"One who smells like a goat."

"Oh. Brutal. Have you ever considered using more... modern insults?"

"Often. I have been tempted to use many on you."

I poked my tongue out at his back, but I was sure that for the first time he was actually joking with me. This was an improvement in our relationship. If you could call the interactions between us over the last few days, or years, a relationship.

We followed the pine needles in silence, along a barren stretch of snowy ground toward the ice cliff.

The longer it took us to trek across the snow, the more I began to worry about the time. It had been easy to ignore it whilst we had been busy, running or shaking funny-colored trees around, but now I was becoming truly anxious. If we didn't find the red shell in time, surely the other Olympians would come and get Poseidon out of here?

"If we don't get the shell, can we find our own way home?"

"This is Apollo's realm, Capricorn, and if this area has been designated for the Trials, then it is entirely possible it is hidden from the view of the rest of Olympus."

Fear pulsed through me at his words. "Hidden from the other gods?"

"Probably, yes."

"But surely Apollo isn't going to give up a bit of his realm just to keep competitors stranded forever?"

Poseidon shrugged. "I would. Our realms are magic, and can accommodate much."

I shook my head, deciding not to comment on the moral questionability of keeping someone prisoner anywhere for eternity.

"Kryvo, how much time do we have?"

"Nine minutes and fifty seconds," he squeaked. Poseidon looked over his shoulder at me.

"The starfish knows the time?"

"Yes."

"How long?"

"Can't you hear him?"

"No. I could hear him when you stuck him to me." His expression darkened, and I understood why Kryvo didn't want to repeat the experience.

"Nine minutes," I said. The flash of concern in Poseidon's eyes was backed up by his quickening pace, and I felt my own feet moving faster.

When we reached the cliff a moment later, we saw that the ice had been carved into, a tall, thin section removed to create a path into the ice. The red needles led straight into it. I couldn't help pausing, despite the pressure of the time. The image of the two enormous, sky-high pieces of ice slipping back together and crushing us to death was impossible to avoid.

Poseidon stepped into the narrow passage though, and I swallowed, jutted out my chin, and followed. The ice reflected so much light that it was hard to see, and I found myself squinting. Not that there was anything to really look at. On our left was the chunk of ice that held the talontaur, and I could see it below us, below the sea-level, dark and slightly warped through the ice at this distance.

The ice on our right was empty, just a sheer lump of clear, cold glittering frozen water.

Or was it?

Something was moving in there. Something small and sparkling. Something red.

"Poseidon!" He turned to me, and I pointed.

"There's nothing there. We must not waste time." He started to turn back.

"I can see the shell! A small red shell, moving around in the ice."

He looked again. "There is nothing there. The trail of pine has not ended. We need to be faster." He turned and broke into a jog.

"But-" I started, but when I looked back at the shell, it was gone. "Shit," I swore, then jogged after the ocean god.

A roar rumbled through the passageway a few seconds later, and I tried not to let my fear still my motion. My first thought was that it was the ice, rumbling as the two colossal chunks moved back together. But I realized quickly that it wasn't. It was the noise of a man.

"Polybotes," hissed Poseidon, ahead of me. The passage was too narrow for two people to stand abreast. I was behind him so couldn't see a thing.

"Where?"

"Ahead."

"No shit," I snapped.

"There is a hole in the floor in a few feet. The shout came from down there."

Sure enough, in a couple of feet Poseidon slowed down, then stepped over a large hole in the ice. Movement caught my eye, and I turned to my right.

Polybotes was inside the ice. And whizzing around him like a damned snitch at a quidditch game was the red shell. He groped for it, but his body was in a space too small for him, and one arm was pinned at his side.

"It's a tunnel." Without another word, Poseidon dropped down into the hole in the ice. A second later, he appeared to my right, inside the ice. Even at his seven feet height, he was half the size of the giant. I watched as he ran toward Polybotes.

But then the red shell stopped flying around the giant's head and moved fast in the opposite direction. It zoomed along the tunnel, straight past Poseidon, and then me, into the left hunk of ice. I expected Poseidon to change direction, following it, but he just kept going toward the giant.

He hadn't seen it, I realized.

I looked down at the hole, knowing, but not willing to do what I needed to do.

"We could hide?" offered Kryvo.

"We're inside a massive transparent block of ice," I told him. "Literally the worst place to hide in the world."

"I'd argue, but you have four and a half minutes."

"Fuck." With a quick prayer, I dropped into the tunnel.

15

ALMI

It was no colder in the tunnel, but the surface beneath my sandals seemed slippier as I ran along the tube after the flying red shell. It was only seconds before I felt queasy. Claustrophobia crushed in on me as I realized that I didn't know how to get back if I got lost. I whirled, trying to see Poseidon, and spotted his dark form through the clear block behind me, engaged with the giant. Were they fighting? I was too far to see clearly.

"Poseidon!" I yelled. "The shell is this way!"

As if on cue, the shell zoomed past my face, tantalizingly close. I reached out for it, closing my fist around empty air just inches from it.

"Damn it!" I pelted after it as it zoomed off, so intent on following it that it was only when the light changed that I realized where I was headed.

The talontaur.

I was right above it, I realized as a dark shape filled the

ice below me. I slowed, looking down, and the blood in my veins felt as cold as the ice I was surrounded by.

Its head was turned up, and its eye was fixed on me. One of its crab-like legs was burrowing up through the ice, straight toward the tunnel I was standing in.

"Almi," I heard Poseidon's voice and whirled gratefully to see him running along the tunnel toward me.

"The shell is here somewhere," I panted.

"We need to get away from the talontaur. Now."

"We need to find the shell!" Poseidon reached me, and I could see stone snaking across the whole left side of his chest, creeping up his neck and along his jaw. Fear coursed through me. A cracking sounded, and we both looked down. The clawed leg had moved further through the ice.

"It's a trap," Poseidon growled.

"The whole frigging Trial is a trap, now help me get the red shell!"

It whizzed between us at my words, taunting us. I reached for it at the same time Poseidon did. He was quicker, but not quick enough. There was a bellow, and movement made me look behind Poseidon. Polybotes was lumbering down the tunnel toward us.

"Move!"

We ran, chasing after the red shell. It doubled back on itself, swooping down within grabbing distance repeatedly, but always quicker than we were.

"Try to catch it with your water," I yelled. Poseidon sent a ribbon of liquid over my head straight at the shell, but it was as though it had hit a waterproof barrier, the liquid dissipating as soon as it hit the shell. It splashed down onto the ground in front of me, and I was too slow to avoid the puddle. My foot slipped and my heart lurched as I lost my footing. I hit the ice hard, accidentally letting go of Poseidon's toga and my momentum causing me to slide on my skirts along the tunnel.

There was another crack as I scrabbled at the ice, trying to slow my movement. One long dark claw burst through the ice ahead of me.

The talontaur had broken through.

"Shit!" I squealed, spinning on my ass but still moving toward the claw.

A roar reverberated through the ice, this one definitely belonging to the monster, and cracks began to appear under my hands. I tried to jam my fingers into them, and the red shell zoomed past my face. Indecision crippled me a moment as I debated lunging for it, and then the world fell away from under me.

I was so shocked I couldn't even scream. The ice I had been sliding on had gone, breaking apart around me. I tumbled through the air, my body twisting so that I could see exactly where I was headed.

Sheer terror surged through me as I looked down into the open jaws of the monster. Poseidon couldn't defeat this thing again without turning to stone.

Something hit my middle, then my fall halted.

A stream of water was winding its way around my middle, lifting me up. The red shell whizzed past my face again, and the creature reared its head back, ready for an attempt to snap at my face.

"Sixty seconds," shrieked Kryvo, his voice barely audible over the sound of my pounding heart.

"Fuck!" I reached out for the shell, fury and desperation filling my whole body, adrenaline coursing through me.

The water holding me lost its tension and I looked up to see Polybotes throwing an almighty punch at Poseidon.

"Bastard shell! Come here! Please, please, please come here!"

I swiped at it as I started to fall again, and to my utter astonishment, something came out of my flailing hand.

I felt a pulse of energy, and a stream of shimmering air flowed from my palm, wrapping itself around the shell. The tiny red object immediately went limp, then came shooting back toward my hand.

"Poseidon!" I screamed as it landed in my palm. "I have the shell. Jump!"

The water tightened around me again, and without hesitation, the sea god jumped from the tunnel. He dropped through the air toward me, pulling on the water rope so that I zoomed up to meet him.

But Polybotes jumped too. Poseidon reached me in mid-air, grabbing my hand and jerking me toward him, just as Polybotes reached us. His weight was too much as he wrapped himself around Poseidon's legs, and together we fell fast.

"Get us out of here!" I shrieked at the shell, as we plummeted toward the open jaws of the talontaur.

16

ALMI

I slammed into something solid, then felt the weight of Poseidon on top of me. All the air left my lungs, and I gasped for breath, but none would come.

You're just winded. Don't panic, said Persephone's voice in my head.

Hands pulled at my shoulders and then I could see as I was dragged upright. We were in Poseidon's courtyard, scores of people on the other side of the gates waving flags and cheering and screaming. Persephone was standing with Galatea and her guards in front of the iron bars and she gave me an encouraging smile along with a cheesy thumbs up as I met her eyes.

Atlas' voice boomed through the air. "The hour is up, for all our competitors. The shells will be counted at a ball graciously hosted by Apollo tonight. Use this time to rest, competitors, for you will get little other chance."

I sucked in air that felt too thick as I clutched my chest, mind reeling. The ground shuddered, and I turned dazedly to see Polybotes stumbling his way to his feet. The giant's eyes met mine, then flicked to my closed fist.

"I nearly got left in there to die," he said, his rumbling voice strained.

I could barely breathe, let alone respond to him.

"Well caught," he said, and my eyebrows shot up in surprise. "If you hadn't got the red shell, we'd all be talon-taur food." With a small nod, he stomped off toward the palace.

"Well caught, indeed." When I turned to Poseidon there was a light in his face I hadn't seen before, and I felt weak for a whole bunch of new reasons. "We need to talk. Now."

I nodded mutely, and took his outstretched hand.

I wasn't at all surprised to find us on the lower level of the pegasi stables when the light from Poseidon's flash cleared.

Warm ocean wind blew across my face, and I finally felt like I could breathe properly. I closed my eyes, taking as long a breath as I could manage, before opening them again and focusing on Poseidon as I let it out. The ocean beyond the tower was calm, the sound of gentle waves and birdcalls soothing my reeling brain.

"I used magic."

Poseidon's eyes were dancing with blue light as he replied. "Yes."

"How?"

He looked down at my chest, and I did the same. The

turquoise in the center of my shell had spread, turning green as the ombre worked its way outward. "Your powers are awakening."

All the adrenaline that had been seeping away surged back through me as I pressed my fingers to my tattoo. "I'll be able to control water now?"

Poseidon shook his head. His bare shoulders were tense, but I didn't think it was with anger or overly severe control this time. "No. Not water. Almi. That was *air* magic."

I stared at him. "What?"

"I felt the power you used, and it wasn't water."

"But... I'm a sea nymph. Like Lily. She had water magic."

"Well, you don't. Those bubbles giving you air to breathe? I think you were doing that. The magical signature was the same."

My mouth fell open. "I was making the bubbles?"

"Yes. I think so."

"No, no this can't be right." Confusion warred with excitement. Magic of any type was a frigging gift. But I was a sea nymph, a creature of the ocean, a citizen of Aquarius. I belonged to the water, surely?

"Almi... Do you realize that you're the reason we're both here? Polybotes was right to thank you. You saved us all." His gaze bore into me, and I realized what the new emotion I was seeing in his face was.

Respect.

"I'm, erm, just better at spotting red stuff than you are, I think," I said awkwardly.

"You are fearless."

I snorted a laugh before I could stop myself. "The fuck am I. I was scared shitless the entire time."

"Yet you faced everything. And drew on a power you didn't even know you had."

He stepped toward me, waves beginning to roll across his irises. "The Oracle is never mistaken."

"What's the Oracle got to do with it?"

The intensity in his expression dropped, and he blinked. "Nothing. We need to test your magic." His words were matter of fact again, the quiet wonder in his tone gone, and he stepped backward.

A huge part of me had hoped he would come all the way, close the gap, and remind me of that torrent of passion and power he had inside him.

"Test it how?"

"Come."

I followed him up the steps to the pegasi pens.

"Blue?" I called the moment we emerged on the higher platform. I heard clopping hooves, then Blue nosed open the stable door of his pen. "Aren't you a sight for sore eyes," I said as he trotted over to me. His golden wings ruffled as he nuzzled at me, and I stroked my hand over his long snout, running my fingers through his blue mane.

"My hair is supposed to be this color," I murmured.

I felt a bit like I was in a dream. The full impact of what I'd done during the ice Trial hadn't really kicked in, though I knew what Poseidon had just said was true. I'd caught the red shell. Without me, we wouldn't have gotten out.

But it was the way I'd caught the shell that was causing the surreal haze buzzing through my mind.

Magic. At long, long, last, I had used magic.

But it was the wrong kind of magic.

"Your affinity with him, and the ship, could be explained by air magic," Poseidon said, nodding his head at Blue.

I turned to the god, raising my eyebrows in question, reluctant to let go of the pegasus. Kryvo gave me more comfort than I could ever have imagined a small slimy starfish could, but the solid bulk and heat of Blue at that moment was what I needed.

Well, what I *really* wanted was the bulk and heat of the moody sea god currently trying to turn my damned world upside-down. But since that didn't appear to be on offer, the flying horse would suffice. "How can I have air magic?"

"I don't know. But it would explain why living under-water all this time didn't awaken it."

I scowled at him, nearly a decade of resentment surfacing involuntarily. "Living underwater all this time?" I repeated angrily. "I lived in the fucking human realm all this time, thanks to you. How much magic do you think was going to surface there?"

He scowled back at me. "The point is that if you have magic now, we can use it."

"We? Huh." I turned back to the pegasus, burying my face in his neck.

Get a grip, Almi, I told myself. *This is not the time to pick a fight.*

You're right. It's not, said Lily, her face forcing its way into my head. *You were unbelievable out there, Almi. And now you have magic. Get whatever help you can from him, before the next Trial starts.*

I breathed in the horsey scent of Blue, and he whinnied softly.

"How do I use it?" I said, as evenly as I could, turning back to Poseidon. His eyes were hard, but he answered me.

"Feel the wind."

"I always feel the wind." Even as I said the words, I realized how true they were. I had always put it down to my slight claustrophobia, always needing to feel fresh air. But what if it was more than that?

"Good. Use it."

I gave him a look. "Use it? Just like that?"

"You did it in the ice."

"We were about to die in the ice. Same as when the bubbles came — I was about to drown. What if I can only use magic when I'm literally about to die?"

Poseidon shrugged. "Then you have less chance of dying."

I let out a long breath. "Not helpful. True, but not helpful."

"I beg to differ. When could access to magic be more helpful than when one is about to die?"

I glared at him. "You said something about testing my magic?"

He held his hand out. With a faint glow, a feather appeared in his palm. It was a plain feather, large and white. I expected the ocean breeze to blow it from his hand, but it stayed exactly where it was.

"Lift the feather. With magic."

I stepped away from Blue. "How?"

"Concentrate," he said.

"You're a terrible teacher," I muttered.

Kryvo's squeaky voice came to me. "He's right, Almi. I think you did make the bubbles yourself. That's air magic. You should try to use it now."

"Do you have better instructions than 'concentrate'?" I asked him quietly. Not quietly enough that Poseidon couldn't hear me, and I saw his face change from confusion to disbelief as he realized I was talking to the starfish stuck to my collarbone.

"Yes. I've been checking the paintings for air magic references since Poseidon mentioned it. You need to imagine that the element you are connected to is surrounding you, then call up enough emotion that it responds. Once it is there, you should be able to make it do as you wish."

I took a deep breath. "Right. I can do this."

I closed my eyes, and tried as hard as I could to feel the breeze moving across my skin. I opened my arms out wide, trying not to feel stupid, and mostly failing.

"Concentrate," I muttered.

The trouble was, I was so used to water, thinking about it, seeing it, pining for a connection to it, that I hadn't spent enough time thinking about air to know what to do.

I called up an image of a tornado in my head, the most air-based thing I could think of.

Almost within seconds of holding the idea, the tornado had taken on a life of its own. I could feel air whipping first around my arms, then my legs, then my whole body, lifting the skirt of my gown, and blasting at my cheeks. When I opened my eyes, I expected the imaginary feeling to drop away, but to my astonishment, my hair *was* snapping around my face, and when I looked down, my skirt was flying around my thighs. Nothing else in the stables was moving though, the flurry of wind contained purely around me.

I let out a bark of delight, and I saw a flash of emotion on Poseidon's face. He held out his palm. "Lift the feather."

I looked at the white feather. *Could you please lift the feather?* I asked the wind that was swirling around me. A slither of air sparked to life, shimmering greeny-blue, then shot toward the feather. Before I could command it to do anything else, it lifted the feather from Poseidon's palm and tossed it out of the stables, into the ocean below. My jaw fell open as the current of air did one little victory lap around Poseidon's head, lifting his loose silver hair from his shoulders, then bolted back to join the rest of the current whirling around me.

Ooh boy. It appeared my magic had a rebellious a streak that outdid mine.

17

ALMI

"Oh!" My utterance fell away as the air turned in one last flurry around me, then vanished, melting away into the ocean breeze.

"Air magic," said Poseidon on an exhale.

"Air magic," I repeated. Thrills were rushing through me, a feeling like no other starting to work its way through all the internal chaos and fatigue. It was a feeling of rightness, a feeling of hope. And not one forced of desperation, like the hope that had kept me going my whole life, but one of true and sincere belief.

When I looked up at Poseidon, I realized I had felt a fleeting glimpse of this feeling before, just one day ago. Standing on the deck of the ship, staring at him.

Perhaps it hadn't been him that had felt so right. Perhaps it had been *me*, standing on the deck of a ship that flew through the air. A ship free from the binding of earth and ocean, designed to soar through the sky. I almost felt giddy when I thought about it.

Another long breath left Poseidon, and his eyes had

taken on that same wild intensity they had last time we were in the stables. But that time, I'd pissed him off.

"Want to go for a ride?" I asked, the question leaving my lips unbidden. Suddenly, all I wanted to do was feel the rush of wind over my face, the boundless freedom of soaring through the sky, just like I had on the ship, but with this new appreciation that was pounding through me.

I hadn't expected him to say yes. But he moved his hand to the little flute on his leather strap, pulled it free, then blew into it. A shrill, off-key whistle echoed through the air, and Blue stamped his feet.

Seconds later, the sound of hooves meeting wood made me spin around.

Another pegasus had landed, and my breath caught.

She was pure gold. Not just her wings, like Blue's, but her whole body; mane, tail — everything. But she looked weightless, her lithe movements so beautifully graceful.

"Oh my god, she's gorgeous."

"She is. She is called Chrysos." His tone was gentle, and I dragged my eyes from the golden pegasus to look at him.

The urge to go to him was almost unbearable.

How could a man be so hard, and yet have a tenderness toward these creatures that turned him into something else completely? Not soft, for sure. But... something else.

Before I could do anything about my inappropriate urges, he had moved to Chrysos, rubbing his hand down her neck, then leaping onto her back like a frigging pro. "You wanted to ride."

His eyes met mine in challenge, a spark in them that had nothing controlled about it at all.

Delicious excitement rose up in me. "How do I get on?" I asked, looking at Blue. Out of nowhere, a gust of wind blew behind me, and I knew what it wanted me to do. I reached up, gripped Blue's neck, and as soon as I jumped, the wind did the rest. It lifted me easily, sliding me onto the pegasus' back as though I had done all the work myself.

I looked at Poseidon gleefully, and the corner of his mouth quirked the tiniest bit.

"Reckon you can keep up?"

"Fuck yes."

Blue bounded for the edge of the stables, and a delighted scream burst from my chest as he launched himself into the air. My skirt flew out, catching like a sail, then pinning to my legs as the pegasus dove toward the waves.

Wind rushed over my face, stinging and strong and so much more energetic than it had ever seemed before.

Gold streaked by me, and I watched in awe as the golden pegasus plunged straight into the sea. She streaked under the surface, her gleaming gold coat and the silver hair of Poseidon visible under the waves as Blue galloped along with them, the salt in the air tangible as the ocean spray reached us.

Poseidon and Chrysos burst up from the water, a jet following them up and corkscrewing around them as they soared high.

"Go, Blue," I urged, and he beat his wings, racing up

after them. Pastel colored clouds filled the sky, coral pinks and soft yellow mingling with pale lavenders and peaches. The higher we got the more I saw little bursts of glittering air, whizzing around like shooting stars.

I was gripping Blue's mane hard, my thighs clamped around his haunches, but I had no fear of falling.

I urged Blue ahead of Poseidon, then called up the image of the tornado again. Wind rushed me, and I made my request of it.

Carry us higher.

There was a blast of warm current, then I heard a shout from Poseidon.

With a burst of speed that elicited a whinny from both pegasi, we were swept upward.

The wind whirled around us, whipping up the calm clouds, and pulling the flying horses to face each other.

My eyes locked onto Poseidon, and my pulse raced as heat swooped through me.

Unbridled joy was written across every inch of his face. Not a hint of control was left, his muscles bulging as he held onto Chrysos, his head thrown back as his hair whipped around his face, and his whole body radiating life.

Take us down, I asked the wind, and squeezed Blue tighter.

"Hold on!" I yelled, and then we were dropping through the sky like bullets.

As though getting in on the game, both Blue and Chrysos tucked their wings in, making our descent even faster. Fresh adrenaline surged through me as we plummeted toward the sea, the recent memory of dropping into the gaping jaws of certain death unavoidable.

As we got close to the water, I realized Blue wasn't pulling up. I took a breath, then called on the bubbles as we plunged into the sea.

They whooshed around my head as we powered through the water, Blue and Chrysos pulling up so that we stayed close to the surface. Chrysos was driving her legs hard, as though she were galloping on the ground, and I assumed Blue was doing the same. She pivoted, twisting so that she was tipping her rider upside down, and Poseidon pressed himself close to her neck.

Blue did the same, and laughter left my lips, until I saw the view. Being upside-down meant I was looking down now, and before us was Aquarius.

The hundreds of connected golden domes glowed beneath us, grand buildings and tall towers reaching the surface just visible. There were scores of animals; whales and dolphins and turtles and rays and eels and many other creatures too small to see, moving around the domes.

Blue righted himself as we soared past the palace stable tower, tipping me the right way again before bursting up through the waves, back into the sky.

I was breathless with excitement as he beat his wings, taking us higher, and I felt a stab of disappointment when he turned toward the stables.

He set us down, and Poseidon and Chrysos landed a beat after we did.

I slipped from his back, my legs leaden and my hands shaking. "Thanks, Blue. That was amazing."

I was wet again, my skirt heavy around my legs and my hair cool on my bare shoulders.

I felt a warm touch on my back, and I turned to Poseidon. He looked more alive than I'd ever seen him.

"You must rest," he said, seeing how unsteady I was.

"Probably. Could I have some more of those vials?"

He held out his other hand, two vials in it. "Could I have the shells?"

I nodded and fished them out of my bra. His gaze fixed on my chest, and his jaw tensed. I dropped the shells into his palm, picking up the vials in their place. "Fair trade," I smiled at him.

"Almi..." There was a strain to his voice that didn't match the restlessness in his eyes. "Why did you come back?"

My own elation dipped. "I told you. To save Lily."

"How were you planning to do that?"

I swallowed. Should I tell him? Was now the time? "I... I heard of a place that had healing powers. I wanted to try to find it."

"What place?"

I bit my lip. "Atlantis."

His eyes darkened instantly, his back stiffening. "The Font of Zoi," he murmured quietly.

"Yes."

He stared at me. "I have no idea how you found out about its existence, but if you know of it, I assume you also know I am its keeper?" I nodded. His jaw twitched. "That's why you came to the palace?"

"Yes."

"You thought to what, woo a trip to the deepest depths of the ocean from me?"

"No. I thought to steal your ship."

His mouth fell open. "You are unbelievable."

I resisted the urge to say something sarcastic. "Have you tried to use the font?"

"I don't know where you got your information from, but Atlantis is no longer accessible." His voice had turned hard, and for the first time since the end of the Trial, I saw tendrils of stone sneaking across his ribs.

"What?"

"It's not an option," he growled.

"But the book says it can heal anything. It could wake Lily up and cure the stone. We have to try!" I could feel fresh hope blossoming at the knowledge that he hadn't already tried to use the Font of Zoi. It could still be the answer.

"The Oracle said the heart of the ocean was the only way to cure the stone blight," he stated, folding his arms across his chest.

"We don't even know what the stupid heart of the ocean is! And besides, what about the sleeping sickness?"

"The Oracle said your sister would sleep until the gods weep. Not until you visited a long hidden, deadly realm," he snapped.

"Well, unless you want to tell me how the fuck I'm supposed to make a god weep, give me a better plan." I glared at him, and a gust of wind whipped around us. Blue and Chrysos both backed up.

"Your power is awakening. We may soon find out what the heart of the ocean is," he said. "That is the plan."

"It's a shit plan," I snapped.

Anger sparked in his eyes, and the sky around the tower darkened. "We have to win these cursed Trials, and then we will cure the blight. Do not presume to know better than an Olympian."

"Why the hell do you think you know more about Nereids and hearts of the damned ocean than I do? I am telling you, we do not have time to wait for this heart to show up!"

"This conversation is over," he snarled.

"Don't you fucking dare—"

But I was too late. Before I could begin to tell him what I would do to him if he flashed me away, I was standing in my bedroom, dripping wet and furious.

18

POSEIDON

She was getting too damn close.

Her face when she had brought the wind to life... Fuck, I'd almost thrown a decade of discipline away right then and there.

She was a damned force of nature, with no fucking concept of control.

I needed her like I needed water.

I wanted her like nothing I'd ever desired before.

Not just her touch, her kiss, her body. But that unbridled tenacity, her fierce courage. She was more than I had ever anticipated she would be, in every way. And I couldn't watch her come into her power any more than I could watch her die.

I had watched her every day for eight years. I'd seen her tears. Seen her grief. Seen her sorrow and loneliness.

I knew what she had thought of me. She believed me to be cold, hard, cruel. Hell, the world believed the same.

But she was starting to see the truth. Every time she looked at me, every time she touched my skin, every time she brought my soul to fucking life…

How could I be so damned stupid?

It had to stop.

It couldn't continue.

Or she would be the death of us both.

19

ALMI

I smoothed down the skirt of my dress, trying not to grind my teeth as I did so.

"Are you alright?" Mov asked. "Do you not like the dress?"

"I love the dress," I told them, trying to smile. "I'd just rather be wearing pants and a shirt."

They scowled at me, before schooling their features again. "Why would you choose pants over this?" Mov gestured at the mirror.

My reflection showed a tight red dress, with a split high enough in the left leg that I could just about run in an emergency. It had puffed shoulder sleeves and a sweetheart neckline, just low enough to show my blossoming shell tattoo. My purple hair had a lot more blue running through it now and had been braided in a fishtail style, the plait placed strategically over my shoulder, hanging almost to my waist. Kryvo was, of course, on the side that wasn't obscured by my braid.

"It's lovely," I reassured Mov. "It's just that last time I

put on a dress, I didn't expect to immediately have to swim, run, fall and a ton of other shit, in it. Pants would have been easier."

"Do you think you are likely to have to compete in this dress?" they asked, frowning.

"I wouldn't rule anything out."

Mov lifted a finger to their lips thoughtfully. They disappeared into a closet, then came out a moment later, holding a black leather belt that was too small for any normal person's waist.

"We can strap a weapon to your thigh?"

Images of badass, sexy women in spy films flooded my brain and I nodded enthusiastically. "Yes. Let's definitely do that."

I had crashed hard when I'd gotten back to my room. Not until after I'd bellowed out some rage in the shower over Poseidon's dismissal of the font in Atlantis. But the anger, on top of everything else, had burned me out fast, and I'd slept long and soundly.

I'd awoken still pissed though. And not just at Poseidon.

The thing I was most pissed about was Atlas.

Atlas and these stupid fucking Trials.

I had magic now. Magic that I wasn't really sure how to control or what to do with, but I had it. It was helping me. Saving my damn life. I was finally ready, finally in with an actual shot at doing something useful for once, and I was stuck facing a load of deadly monsters for the entertainment of a lunatic god instead of saving Lily.

. . .

"I wonder what Poseidon did to Atlas' wife?" I mused aloud as the nymphs bustled about in the closet.

The more my confused feelings roiled around for the ocean god, the more I longed to know the answer to that question.

I had a connection to Poseidon, and I fundamentally struggled to believe he was cruel or unkind. Hard, sometimes misguided, and a tad merciless perhaps. But a lack of mercy was not the same as cruelty. Mercy could be learned. Or earned. Cruelty was inherent. In the blood. Unfixable.

Kryvo's voice reached me. "I found something in the palace about Atlas."

"About his wife?" My pulse quickened.

"Yes. Do you want to see?"

"Absolutely."

My vision clouded, and then I was looking at a domed ceiling, painted with an obscenely detailed image of what looked like a wedding.

Atlas' wedding, I realized, as I peered at the groom. Hera stood before them at the altar, her dark skin and peacock-colored headdress vibrant in the painting. I scanned the rows of attendees, and spotted Poseidon immediately. Zeus was by his side, and even in the painting, he looked bored. On the right side of the image were gods who weren't Olympians. Titans. So this must have been before the Titonamchy; the war that divided the great gods.

Jeez, that meant whatever had happened between the two of them had happened a long time ago.

I looked back to Poseidon, noticing his clenched fists and moody expression. That could mean nothing, though, I wouldn't have expected him to be the life and soul of a party.

The vision faded, and I bit back my disappointment. "Is that all there is?"

"I can keep looking." Kryvo sounded disappointed, and I hurried to console him.

"That was great," I enthused. "I just wish we knew what happened."

"Well, I don't know why Poseidon has a painting of Atlas' wedding in his palace at all," said the starfish.

"That's a really good point," I said with a frown. "Where is the painting?"

"The north-east wing. It's not used much by anyone except staff."

When the nymphs had finished working their magic, Galatea strode into the dressing room.

"Hey," I said, surprised by how happy I was to see her. "How's it going?"

"I am pleased you got out of the Trial alive," she said.

"Yeah. You and me both."

"I have been trying to find out how Atlas has so thoroughly infiltrated the palace."

"And? You find anything?"

"No." Galatea gestured for me to follow her, so I did. She marched along the corridors like she would know where she was headed even if she were blindfolded, and I wondered how long she had lived in the palace.

That thought made another spring to mind. "How old are you?"

She cast a look at me. "That is an impolite question."

"People keep telling me I'm impolite. I may as well live up to expectations," I shrugged.

She gave me a small scowl, then she shrugged, too. "Four hundred."

"Woah," I said. "And how many of those years have you spent here?"

"Almost all of them. Poseidon found me when I was very young."

"Found you?"

"Yes. We do not have time for my tales now, I am afraid. We are expected at Apollo's ball."

I screwed my face up. "What is it with you guys and balls?"

Galatea gave me a sympathetic look. "I do not care for them either, in truth." I took in her tight fighting garb and severe face and found myself unsurprised.

"Not a fan of twirling around on the dancefloor?"

"I would rather run rings around my enemies," she said.

I nodded. "Cool."

She frowned at me. "What does the temperature have to do with balls or enemies?"

"Nothing. Ignore me."

"So odd," she muttered, then resumed her strides toward a large, sweeping staircase carpeted in red. "The gods like balls and ceremonies because it gives them a chance to show off and size each other up," she said. "They love drama. Can't get by without it. There's nothing worse for an immortal than boredom."

"Where are Hera and Aphrodite? They haven't been at the last few gatherings."

"Hera has been missing for a while. Zeus fled Olympus, and it appears she has chosen him over the others." Her tone was clipped.

"Well, she is his wife."

"That matters not, when the moral choice is clear. Hera is a woman of integrity."

"And insane jealousy, if I remember correctly?" I muttered.

"On occasion, yes. But she is one of the better gods."

"From what Atlas said, she told him about my marriage to Poseidon so that he could seek revenge. I've got to be honest, she's not top of my list right now."

"Yes. That is troubling."

"Troubling. Yeah. I was going more for 'fucking inconvenient'. But troubling works too."

We reached the top of the staircase, where a massive archway led into a beautiful room I recognized immediately as Poseidon's throne room.

Poseidon stood from his throne, and I was surprised to see his ocean-toga.

"I thought I'd lost that," I said, staring.

"It is not a normal toga. It is enchanted," he said. "You are no longer angry with me?"

"Oh no, I'm still mad. I just got distracted for a second."

I was almost certain I saw a twitch of amusement in his face, which only made me more determined to remember I was annoyed with him.

"I have not seen you in red before."

I blinked. "You've spent like, six days with me. Most of which I was wearing brown and white."

"Yes."

I lifted my hands up. "That's it?"

"Yes."

"Jeez, and you say I'm the odd one."

"You've got to be odd to be number one," he said, his voice only just audible. I snapped my eyes to his, sparks surging through me. Why? Why would him quoting my own bullshit back at me cause such a physical reaction?

Because he thinks you're funny. Lily's voice in my head sounded amused. *And that makes you happy.*

Funny? He doesn't think anything is funny! I've seen him smile once!

And what would you do to see him smile again?

Anything.

The answer forced its way through any mental blocks I had with ease.

Fuck. Would I really do anything?

He stepped down from his throne toward me, oozing grandeur and power and cool stoicism. All things I had zero interest in. But his eyes... I was sure I could see raw, wild emotion deep in there, disguised as fierceness, carefully contained and locked away.

"When we are in Apollo's realm, you need to be wary of a number of things," he said.

"Apollo?" I suggested.

Poseidon shook his head. "No. He is cocky and somewhat overly jovial, but in your public position, you need not fear him. He is at war with the vampires right now, though. And they are certainly to be feared."

My jaw dropped. "Did you just say vampires?"

"Yes. Women who live by consuming warm blood."

"Well, shit. I didn't know Olympus had those."

He frowned. "All life began in Olympus. The ancient word for them is *lamia*. They have evolved much since the ancient times though."

"Why is Apollo at war with them?"

"He is the god of the sun," he answered, as though that made it obvious. Before I could ask him to elaborate, he was talking again. "Atlas will not be pleased that we were able to flout his attempts to separate us, or beat the ice Trial. It is of the utmost importance that you avoid him at all costs."

I nodded. "That's not a hard command to follow. He creeps me out."

"He has a lot of anger."

I couldn't help taking the opening. "Want to tell me why he hates you so much?"

"No. We only have a few minutes more until we will be flashed there. Do you have the vials I gave you?"

"Yes."

"Good. I strongly suspect that we will be sent to the earth Trial straight from the ball." His eyes roamed down my dress, and I was sure they lingered a little longer than was necessary on my exposed leg. I pointed my toe and bent my knee, like a burlesque dancer.

"That's why I got the split. So that I could run," I said in a mock sultry voice.

When he looked at me, his eyes were blazing with heat, and I gulped, tucking my leg back into my skirt immediately.

Galatea coughed behind me, and I felt my face flush.

"You're a leg man, huh?" I whispered awkwardly.

"Do not test me," he growled.

I hadn't realized what a test my leg was for him.

Or how much his reaction would please me.

I told you, said Lily. *You want him to want you.*

Before I could argue with my imaginary sister, the world flashed white.

ALMI

The first thing I noticed was the glittering sheen of frost covering everything. We were in an outdoor courtyard, tall statues and Grecian fountains adorning the mosaic tiles, and creeping vines and purple wisteria winding around interspersed stone columns. The area was lit by hundreds of tiny floating lights, which shone just brightly enough to catch the sparkling frost that covered every single surface.

People milled around everywhere, many faces familiar now from the last few gatherings. I spotted Kalypso immediately, as she was only standing a few feet away, talking with an exceptionally handsome man with dark, dreadlocked hair, and a chest as broad as some of the gods.

"Where are we?" I asked Poseidon, but I got no answer. I turned and realized he'd already gone. Galatea gave me a vaguely sympathetic look. "I think you spooked him," she said.

"How?"

She pointed to my leg. "With that."

Before I could answer, Persephone came toward us, laying a hand on my shoulder and squeezing it. "You did so fucking well in that Trial!" Without even considering the action, I leaned forward and hugged her. The movement may have taken me by surprise, but she didn't seem fazed at all. She returned my embrace, then held me at arm's length, giving me a grinning once over.

"You don't look like you're in need of any healing. In fact, you look great."

I shook my head. "Thank you. Something amazing happened." Excitement fizzed through me as she leaned in, eyebrows raised in question. She was wearing a black gown with grassy-green trim across the low-cut front, and a tiara made from golden roses donned her white hair. She looked like someone from a movie or a video game, and normally, I would be intimidated by someone as beautiful as she was, but I trusted her instinctively.

Galatea moved closer so that she could hear me.

"I have some magic now," I whispered, and touched my fingers to my shell tattoo.

"That's great! Does that mean the heart of the ocean will show up?"

"That's what Poseidon is hoping. What it definitely means is that I can breathe underwater."

Galatea let out a sigh of relief. "Thank the gods for that," she said.

"For sure."

A nymph arrived with a tray of drinks, and we all took one. It was the same delicious fizzy wine as before, and I sipped gratefully.

"Where are we?" I asked.

Persephone held out her hand and gestured her head toward some railings at the edge of the courtyard. "Come see."

I took her hand and we walked across a neatly manicured lawn shining with frost. "Apollo is the god of the sun, so parts of his realm are intolerably hot. In order to balance that out, he has most of the rest of his realm made from ice."

We reached the stone railings and I peered over the edge.

We were on the top of a sheer cliff of ice. Water met the ice at the bottom, and was completely frozen over.

I looked at Persephone. "Is this where the Trial was?"

She nodded. "Yeah. We're on top of the ice cliff you guys were in."

"What about the talontaur?" Fear zipped through me, making my muscles tight.

"Hades said it's been moved. I don't know where, but look." She turned and pointed in turn to Hades, Artemis, Athena, Hephaestus and Dionysus. They were the only Olympians in our line of sight, all drinking and talking with creatures that looked like they had been invented by somebody on drugs. All except Hephaestus, who was staring glumly over the railings, nothing but an enormous leather apron covering his hulking torso. "With this many all-powerful beings here, you can relax."

"There are some all-powerful beings here that do the opposite of make me relax," Galatea growled, and I saw who her gaze was fixed on.

"Atlas." He was standing by a fountain with a very

pretty woman with neon blue skin and hair, and Ceto. Both Atlas and Ceto turned briefly our way, before resuming their conversation. Ceto's slimy octopus legs writhed on the tiles, her skin just like that of the rotbloods, lava-like ripples moving over her body.

Man, she creeped me out so much worse than the rest of them.

"There are some pretty powerful lamia here too," said Persephone, frowning. "They come from the Underworld originally - I had to fight an empousa once." She shuddered. "Fucking terrifying creatures. Anyway, Hades has been talking to Apollo a lot recently about the hostilities with the vampires. He can't control them once they leave the Underworld."

I was about to ask more, but a familiar face materialized in the crowd, and I gasped. "Silos!"

I rushed forward as he spotted me, a huge grin taking his face as he pushed past people to reach me. He wrapped his arms around me in a hug.

"Silos! How did you get here?"

"Dad." He beamed. "Almi, look at you!"

I did a twirl, and he laughed. "Ever think you'd see me in a dress?" I asked.

"Nope. But I'm glad I have. It suits you." His tone was soft, and I smiled at him.

"Thanks. And thanks for cheering me on. I saw you before."

"Are you serious? Of course I'm cheering you on! I can't believe you're Poseidon's *wife*. When the fuck were you going to mention that?"

I cocked my head, giving a small shrug. "You know I'd have told you if I could."

He nodded. "Yeah. Why did he make you live in the human world if you were married?"

"To keep me away from other people."

Silos frowned, then looked nervously over his shoulder, tensing. "Is he the jealous type? Do I need to keep my distance?"

I laughed. "Honestly, I'm just a business transaction to him. He needs me for something the Oracle at Delphi told him about. There's no jealousy in this marriage," I assured him.

His shoulders relaxed. "I can't believe you've almost been eaten by sea monsters twice."

I was happy he'd changed the subject. I didn't know what it meant that I'd much rather talk about nearly dying than Poseidon, but that appeared to be the case.

"I know. How's Lily?"

"The same." Compassion shone in his big brown eyes.

"I'm close now," I said. "I'm going to save her, Silos."

He nodded. "If anyone can, it's you."

I smiled at him, until a fizzing electric feeling rippled across my skin. I knew what it was, I'd felt it numerous times before now.

"Atlas," I murmured, turning and looking for the Titan. But I couldn't see him anywhere. Why had he sent that feeling? To let me know he was watching me? Just venting some anger at us for surviving today? Poseidon had said to be wary of him.

I looked back at Silos. "I have some pretty messed up

enemies here now," I told him. "It might be safer for you to keep your distance from me."

He opened his mouth, then closed it again, thinking.

"You know," he said eventually. "I'm going to guess you have a reason for saying that, and go with it. But Almi, if you need anything, or I can help you in any way…"

"Silos, you are helping me more than anyone in the world by keeping Lily safe. I owe you everything."

He smiled again, then hugged me.

"Keep kicking ass, Almi."

"You betcha."

ALMI

"Who is he?" asked Galatea when I returned to the two women.

"My friend from when I was a kid. He's been taking care of my sister for me. Ever since Poseidon sent me away." Seeing Silos had forced out some of my new, softer feelings toward the ocean god, and reminded me of just what he had put me and Lily through.

"Do you still want me to visit your sister?" asked Persephone, voice gentle.

"Yes! Oh my god, yes, I would love you to," I told her. "The next time we get a long enough break from these Trials, I would be so grateful if we could go to her."

I didn't think Persephone could cure her, but I couldn't see how it could hurt. Any information would be useful, as would any slowing down of the process.

"Of course. Just use that rose I gave you to let me know you need me. Hephaestus made it for me. Well," she said, frowning. "Hades asked Hephaestus to make it for me. He's a little… shy around women."

"Isn't he married to like, the ultimate woman, Aphrodite?"

Anger sparked in Persephone's eyes. "Don't talk to me about that witch," she spat.

"Now, now," chided a male voice, deep and lyrical. "You mustn't speak ill of the Olympians." Apollo appeared beside us with a shimmer of gold. And gold was the only word I could think of as I took him in. His tousled golden hair flopped down over gleaming golden eyes. His toga too was gold, and fastened with a huge, golden, lyre brooch.

"Good evening, Apollo," Persephone said.

He threw a brief but devastating smile at her, then locked his eyes on me.

"You, Almi, are very, very interesting. Who knew the old water goat had a wife?"

I shifted uncomfortably. "Well, the whole world knows now."

"You are a sea nymph, yes?" I nodded. "Then…. Why do you have air magic?"

My stomach clenched, both with excitement and nerves. "You can feel my magic?"

"Sugar, I'm an elemental weather god. Of course I can."

I swallowed. "I'm only just learning how to use it," I admitted. Poseidon had said that Apollo wasn't a threat, and if he could feel my magic, there wasn't much point lying to him.

He grinned at me, and my chest tightened. He was frigging beautiful. Not in the same way as Poseidon — not at all. Poseidon was solid-mass-of-deep-and-mysterious-power kind of beautiful whereas Apollo was joyous-to-look-at kind of beautiful.

"Want a tip?"

"Sure."

"You can't control air. It is almost as wild as the ocean, and it may not be as strong or powerful, but everything relies on it. *Everything*. It has all the power."

I blinked at him. "I can't control it?"

"Nope. Don't even try. If you can win over the wind, you'll have an ally for life, but you can't bend air to any will."

I tried to process his words. "So, how do I—"

Before I could finish my question, he was gone, striding toward two women with tree bark for skin and green hair.

"Air magic?" Galatea was staring at me like I'd grown a second head.

"Yeah. Apparently."

"But... You're a Nereid."

"Yup." I wrung my hands and she continued to gape at me, confusion written across her face.

"If it keeps you alive, who gives a shit what kind of magic it is?" Persephone said.

I looked at her gratefully. "Yes. Exactly. Magic is magic, right?"

"Wrong." Galatea frowned. "Air magic is not of Aquarius."

Discomfort rolled through me. "Well, I am. I don't know how this has happened, but it has. And my shell is coloring. That happens to Nereids when they get their power, so… Even though I might still be broken, I *am* a Nereid."

I was speaking overly defensively, and I tried to relax. But Galatea's reaction was a mirror of my own worst thoughts.

What if I wasn't a Nereid? Which would mean… Lily wasn't really my sister.

Persephone threw a glare at Galatea as she laid her hand on my shoulder again. "Look, we all come into our own in different ways. Just because you're the first to do something one way, doesn't mean it's the wrong way. It's just… new."

"Or odd," I sighed, but her words forced their way through my paranoia. "Thanks," I told her, hoping my sincerity came across. "You're being really kind to me."

"People here are kinder than you think they are," she smiled. "And besides, it's true."

"I'll try to believe that."

"I am not trying to be unkind," said Galatea, her face still conflicted, but less accusatory. "I am sorry. I just find it confusing that the King of the Ocean would marry a being not of water."

"I don't think he knew at the time. In fact, I know he didn't. We both found out today."

"Air is a powerful element, like Apollo said," Galatea said, straightening. "I am sure you can command much respect with it."

"Command respect? Galatea, I'm not hankering after a general's job like yours. I want to survive this bullshit and cure my sister. Ideally, getting rid of this fucking stone thing altogether if we can. But I'm not after respect."

"You are a queen."

"You were the one who told me that would never happen! I specifically remember you telling me not to get my hopes up."

"That was before…" she gestured vaguely in the air, then pointed at my leg. "Before that."

"What?"

"Almi, I have never, ever seen him look at a woman like he did you. I have never seen his control so close to the edge. And I have been by his side for centuries."

My brain stuttered to an unhelpful halt. "What?"

Persephone gave a small, tinkling chuckle. "Do you fancy him?"

I turned to her, mouth open. "Look at him! How in the name of all things holy am I supposed to find him *unattractive?*"

She smirked at me.

"That doesn't mean I like him, though! He kept me from my only family for almost a decade! He's frigging miserable — which, I might point out, is the last quality I would look for in a guy, and on top of that, he's got me wrapped up in these bullshit Trials by doing something to another man's wife! I am not fucking interested."

I folded my arms over my chest and wished I hadn't spoken so loudly as the two women stared at me.

"Sure, you're not," said Persephone eventually, before taking a long sip of her drink, then holding up her empty glass. "Do you want another one?"

"Yes."

Neither woman brought up Poseidon again, which I was grateful for. Something I was also grateful for was the opportunity to ask about the other guests for the first time. Both Persephone and Galatea seemed happy to answer my questions about the different species and types of creatures.

The courtyard was beautiful, and though the sparkling frost covered the statues and the neat little trees, there was no chill in the air at all. The twinkling fairy-lights made it feel festive, and I found myself starting to relax. The absence of Atlas concerned me a little, but it definitely made things less tense, not having to watch for him. I had caught glimpses of Poseidon, here and there, talking to different folk. But he had avoided my eye, and I had done the same.

An area in the middle of the garden was made up of large square marble tiles, and people were dancing across them to music played by a woman plucking the golden strings of an enormous, gilded harp. She looked utterly lost in the tune, her fingers flying over the tight strings.

"She's a muse," Persephone said. "Fuck knows which one, there's like, nine, or something."

"And what is the grey thing that makes me want to drown myself?" I asked, pointing at the sea foam creature I'd seen the first night I'd arrived at the palace.

"That's an aphros," said Galatea. "I'm not a big fan of them myself. But they're an important part of Aquarius."

I was about to ask why, when someone started screaming. We all whirled, looking for the source of the noise. People began moving somewhere off behind the dancefloor, where the trees were thicker and there were fewer twinkling lights. I saw a glimmer of gold slither across the ground, disappearing into the undergrowth. A snake?

Persephone began to move quickly toward the commotion, and Galatea and I followed.

"What happened to him! Why is he like this?" a woman's voice was sobbing. My chest tightened, anxiety washing through me.

"No, this can't be… This is the man you arrived with tonight?"

"Yes, of course it is! He's my husband!" the woman half-shrieked back. Persephone pushed through the gathered guests, and when I squeezed through after her, I stumbled to a halt.

A merwoman, with matte white hair and green skin, was hanging from the arm of a statue. A statue of a merman. Tears streaked her face, and her chest was heaving as she sobbed.

"One minute, he was asking me to dance, and the next…" She broke down, sinking to her knees but not letting go of the statue's hand.

Sorrow welled up through me, edged with a colossal bout of fear.

The stone blight.

Poseidon had managed to keep it a secret so far. I scanned the faces of the crowd, looking for him, and not having to look for long. Folk parted instantly as he and Hades moved toward the woman and the stone edifice that used to be her husband.

Poseidons' face blanched as he took in the scene.

He turned to the assembled crowd. "Please, go back to the ball. This will be fixed, forthwith."

Nobody argued, and I knew why. A deep need to obey him thrummed through me, so against my own nature that I knew it was of a divine source.

I found myself taking a step back, before Persephone grabbed my forearm, holding me in place.

Everybody dissipated, and my new friend hurried to the grieving woman. She laid her hand on her arm as she ducked down to her, and the woman's sobs abated straight away.

"Sire," said Galatea, stepping to Poseidon.

"Take him to the palace, with the others." Poseidon's voice was hard, as hard as the man turned to stone before us.

For a split second, I considered objecting. I knew what came next. Poseidon would make her forget about him. But as I watched the woman being soothed by Persephone, abject grief in her face, I wondered how awful it would be for someone to take away her pain.

It would only be temporary.

But would it?

What if we failed to cure the blight? What if this merman existed as a statue for the rest of his life?

What if Lily became a statue?

"If we fail, you have to make them remember." I said the words out loud, and I wasn't even sure I was close enough for Poseidon to hear them, but his eyes snapped to mine.

"They will feel the pain all over again." His voice was as quiet as mine was, but I heard him clearly.

"Yes. But if their loss is permanent, it belongs to them. They need closure. They need their memories."

He gazed at me a long moment. "Granted." I raised my eyebrows, not fully sure what he meant by the word. "Your request is granted," he clarified gently.

A bubble of sadness coiled up through my center, rooting in my throat. "Thank you."

A thundering boom made everyone jump in surprise, and a few people cry out.

"What's that?" someone asked.

I already knew though. I could almost taste the unsettling electricity tang of Atlas' magic.

The crowd parted, revealing the Titan standing in the middle of the dancefloor, ten feet tall and wearing a white toga adorned with his interlocking ring sigil.

"Citizens of Olympus, esteemed gods," he boomed, bowing his head. "Are you enjoying yourself?"

Nobody answered him. I strongly suspected that nobody wanted him to win. The Olympians may be a little batshit crazy, but this guy? He was frigging nuts.

"Oh, I see you have experienced a little tragedy over there." He looked at the stone merman, and made a mock pout. "I don't believe he was anyone important, so best not to dwell on it."

Anger surged through me.

"Now, let me relieve you of your boredom! It's time to see how our contestants performed in the last Trial."

Ceto, Kalypso and Polybotes all melted out of the crowd, coming to stand in front of him. Poseidon and I stayed exactly where we were.

A flame dish shimmered into being before the Titan,

the flames leaping high, then showing five glass vases. There were little shells in the bottom of four of them.

"Polybotes, one shell." The giant grunted as a shell appeared in the bottom of one the vases.

"Kalypso, four shells." I raised my eyebrows as she smiled, and four shells appeared in a vase that already had three in it.

"Ceto, three shells." Her vase filled higher.

"Almi, three shells."

"Wait, what—?" I tried to interrupt, but he spoke louder.

"Poseidon, no shells." The empty vase in the image remained empty, whilst three shells appeared beside my existing one.

"No, they're his!" I shouted. Atlas turned to face me.

"The shells are counted at the moment the red shell is used. All three shells were on your person, my little queen."

The way he said the word queen somehow made me feel sick, and I glared at him. "You're a rotten fucking—"

Before I could finish, he roared again, turning back to the audience at large. "And now, let's really spice things up. Off we go, to the next Trial."

"Jackass!" I bellowed, as we were flashed away from the ball.

ALMI

I was so furious when I opened my eyes under the water that I almost forgot to hold my breath.

I willed the bubbles to come to me, almost as desperate for the air so that I could fume about Atlas as to actually breathe.

The swirl of bubbles rushed toward me out of nowhere, whizzing around my face until I could see through it clearly.

Thank you, clever new air magic, I thought as I drew a breath and looked around myself, trying to find Poseidon.

My surroundings were significantly different to last time. The first thing I noticed was that the water was warm. The second thing I noticed was green. Green everywhere.

I was in some sort of underwater meadow. The entire ground below me—which I could see easily because the water was so crystal clear—was covered in a richly green, fluffy moss. Moss-covered boulders and huge plants lined the areas to either side of me, creating a channel.

My heart skipped a little when I used my arms to turn myself in a circle. I couldn't see Poseidon.

"Kryvo?"

"I'm here."

"Do you know anything about where we are?" I could recall what Atlas had said about tropical seagardens, but the little starfish might know more.

"Aphrodite's realm, Pisces, is made up of many small tropical islands, and I think we are in the channels running between them that are dedicated to her under-water plants."

"Okay. What's going to try to kill us here?"

"Pretty much all of the plants."

"Right."

"And Kalypso is in here with us somewhere. I would say she is pretty dangerous too."

"Agreed."

Feeling glad that I'd drunk all of Poseidon's vial before the ball and that his suspicion that we would be sent straight here from the party had been anticipated, I began to swim. I went with the faint current, rather than against it, hoping that was the right thing to do.

"Poseidon!" I called out. Making a noise would draw Kalypso's attention to me if she was nearby, but I figured it was worth the risk. I needed the ocean god with me.

I wasn't sure if that need was driven by fear of surviving without his help, or just wanting to be in his presence. I would have been lying if I didn't admit that he was starting to take up an extraordinarily large amount of space in my thoughts.

I rolled onto my back as I swam, so I could look up at the surface. I was only a few meters under the water, and for a moment, I was tempted to swim up and pop my head out, to see if that gave me any clues. But there was so much happening under the surface I decided I was more likely to find shells, and Poseidon, staying down.

The channel I was swimming along was curving gently, and I could see lots of brightly colored fish flitting about over the tops of the high boulders that made up the sides. When I rounded the corner, my eyes widened.

Opening before me was a landscape of mountains and valleys, all carpeted in thick, green seagrass. Tiny bubbles clung to the grasses before rippling to the surface, making the enormous bowl of water fizz before me. There were plants scattered amongst the green peaks as big as cars. Giant yellow plumed mushroom shaped things caught my gaze first, because they were so vivid in color. But there were patches where purple grasses, dotted with white flowers, lay like rugs over the green, and blue flowers in tall tubes like bluebells shot up between sturdier looking vines.

Between the vastness of the area, the fizzing in the water, and the gentle current, movement was everywhere. Instinct made me force out some of the calm beauty of the place and remember that this was a Trial designed to kill me. But my eyes flitted from one place to another, and I had no idea where to even start looking for shells.

I felt something behind me, my foot brushing something solid. I whipped the knife from my thigh-strap as I spun around, brandishing it in panic.

"It's me." Poseidon hovered in the clear water, his ocean toga looking too bold and blue in the green water world.

"Thank god. This place is immense," I said, on a small a sigh of relief.

"It will not be easy to find shells. Just about every one of these plants is lethal. This is Aphrodite's pet project." His voice sounded thick and gurgled, but it was easier to make out his words than it had been under the ice.

"Like a deadly underwater greenhouse."

He looked at me, then at the dagger in my hand. "You came armed this time."

"Yes."

"Good."

He swam past me, leaving the tributary and moving out over into what I was now terming 'the bowl' in my head.

I followed him, tucking the knife back into the band around my thigh and relishing the badass vibe it gave me.

It really did feel like I was swimming over mountains, the shapes of the green below me undulating and rolling exactly as the ranges had on Sagittarius. I wondered what the place would smell like, if we weren't underwater.

Poseidon swam low, dipping into one of the valleys, and I mimicked him. The air fizzing off the grasses intensified the deeper we went, and I got the distinct memory of being in a bath with a bath-bomb. Ahead, at the lowest point of the vividly bright valley, was a plant. It was as tall as Poseidon, standing alone and bold, and I recognized it immediately.

A Venus fly trap.

Except it was bright violet in color, and had a few... extras.

When we got closer, I could see the two halves of its leaf-shaped jaws were wide open, and the inside of them were baby pink. Instead of thin veined leaves, the plant looked thick and leathery, an almost hide-like texture covering its surface.

Lying in the middle of the lower leaf was a little white shell. Poseidon moved closer, and I grabbed his bare calf.

Tingles moved through my arm at the contact, and I let go quickly as he turned to me.

"It's a trap," I said.

"Clearly."

I pulled a face at him, and he ducked down, swimming to the grassy riverbed. He tugged up a handful of long grass, then swam back up.

Unlike the Venus fly traps I'd seen before, this plant didn't have the little spiny teeth-like protrusions around the edges of its leaves. In fact, there was very little that was threatening about it all, other than the jaw-like shape of the two thick leaves.

Poseidon swam over the top of it, then sprinkled the handful of grasses onto the lower leaf.

Teeth, actual ivory teeth, burst up from each leaf - not just around the edge but over the whole surface. The top leaf came slamming down onto the bottom one, mincing the grass into tiny shreds. Slowly, the leaf-jaws eased open again, the whole plant swaying slightly in the water.

"I don't like it," said Kryvo in a small voice.

"Me neither," I told him. "We're going to need something better than grass to get the shell."

I saw a ribbon of water come from Poseidon's palm, and shoot toward the shell. The second it brushed against the leaf though, the jaw slammed shut, squishing his water ribbon and making it dissipate.

Air? I projected my tentative thought. *Wanna have a go?*

Nothing happened.

I thought about how the wind had tossed the feather off the side of the stables and then ruffled Poseidon's hair earlier that day.

Poseidon's water can't get the shell, but I bet you can.

A corkscrew of tight bubbles whooshed through the water toward me, forming from the tiny fizzing bubbles coming off the grass.

A smile sprang to my lips, despite the seriousness of the situation.

"Well, hello!" I said aloud as the stream of air spiraled around me. "You have to touch only the shell, not the leaves," I told it.

Slowly at first, then more quickly, the air flowed over to the plant.

With a lightning fast dart of movement, the stream zoomed for the shell. The plant snapped shut and I held my breath as the stream whooshed back to me.

It had missed.

As the plant folded open again, I saw the shell still firmly on the leaf. Poseidon looked at me, then his ribbon of water snaked back to the trap.

Poseidon tried another three times, but to no avail. The plant was simply too quick.

"Come on, air," I told it. "One more go. We can do it."

I swam over the top of the massive plant, as close to it as I dared to get. It could easily trap my entire body between its leaf-jaws, piercing me a hundred times with all those lethal teeth.

The stream of air moved more slowly this time, almost creeping through the water toward the shell.

"Slowly," I whispered, as it got within an inch.

Both the stream and I froze as the leaf gave a tiny ripple, then stilled again.

"Super slowly," I breathed, and the stream moved again. Poseidon was watching, a few feet from me, but I tried to ignore him, focusing on the air. Millimeter by painful millimeter, it got closer to the shell. My pulse raced, and I would definitely have been sweating if we had been on dry land. My hands were clenched into fists, my nails digging into my palms as the air finally touched the shell.

The plant's jaw snapped closed, the teeth bursting out ready to impale the intruder.

But my stream of air zoomed back toward me with gusto, spinning me in circles with its strength in the water.

I squealed, and it slowed. I felt something pushing at my hand, cool and firm. When I looked down, the stream of air had turned narrow, trying to pry open my fist. I stretched out my fingers and the air dropped the little shell into my palm.

"Oh my god! You're amazing!"

The air stream started moving again, whizzing me around in another circle and almost making me drop the shell. "Woah!" I laughed. It stopped, instead forming a foot high whirlpool before me, bouncing in the water. "Thank you, very much," I beamed at it, before turning to Poseidon.

He eyed the little whirlpool warily, before swimming over to me. I held out the shell. "You'd better take this," I said.

Light sparked in his eyes, then he reached out, taking the shell and stowing it in a concealed pocket in his toga.

"Does your emotional support starfish have a time check?" he asked me, once the shell was safe.

"Kryvo?"

"Forty-six minutes," Kryvo squeaked.

Poseidon nodded and swam up the valley edge.

"You're welcome," I muttered, swimming after him.

23

ALMI

When we emerged from the valley back out into the bowl, I was happy to let Poseidon take the lead. We swam for what felt like ages, almost everything I saw carpeting the ground below us bright green.

"I've been looking for any other starfish in the palace with views of deadly water plants," Kryvo said.

"Any luck?"

"Yes. A few. I'll let you know if they become relevant."

"What would I do without you, huh?"

"I doubt you would hide," he grumbled.

Eventually, the green under us started to change, as a vivid pink colored weed snaked its way through the grasses. After a few more meters it had smothered everything, turning the riverbed mountains completely pink.

I dipped closer to it, trying to look carefully for shells, or anything that could contain a shell. But if there were any there, they were too well hidden for me to spot.

Poseidon dipped suddenly ahead of me, and I assumed he had found something.

I swam toward him excitedly, then slowed.

He was down amongst the pink weeds, but not digging for a shell, like I thought he would be. The weeds were wrapped around his middle, trying to pull him down to the bottom. His hands were glowing as he swiped at them, but the weeds were too fast, turning him this way and that, and pinning his arms completely to his sides.

Why hadn't he blasted them off with magic already?

Worry filled me as I started to speed up again, but then I saw the dark-skinned figure of Kalypso, ten feet away. She wasn't being dragged down by the weeds — she was too high up. But she was holding her hand out, and I could just make out a rippling in the water coming from her palm, directed straight at Poseidon.

I pulled my knife from my leg band and sped toward him. As soon as I reached his thrashing form I began to hack at the weeds, but the dagger barely moved through them.

"In my toga," Poseidon snarled, and tried to turn toward me. A pink weed snaked its way around my wrist, and I snapped my hand back, trying to keep my body high above Poseidon's. Weight was crushing down on me though, a strong current of water pushing me. As the current moved over my face, the bubbles providing me air slowed, then vanished.

Shit.

I held my breath, reaching into the top of Poseidon's toga, where I knew he kept his dagger strapped to his chest.

Alarm at my lack of air and the pressure from Kalypso's magic distracted me from the spark I got when my fingers brushed his chest, and I tugged the dagger out.

It was significantly sharper than mine, and I sliced through the weeds in seconds.

Free, Poseidon burst up, soaring through the water straight at Kalypso.

She rose to meet him, and glowing currents crashed into each other between them as they both fired water magic at each other.

My bubbles whooshed back around me as Kalypso's magic was redirected, and I drew in a grateful breath.

Something brushed my ankle and I looked down, lifting my knees high in the water when I saw that it was a pink weed, reaching for me.

"Oh no you don't," I told it. I looked over at the fight between the two ocean gods. If Poseidon used too much power, he would turn to stone again. I had to help.

Air? Fancy sending Kalypso somewhere far away from here?

The tiny bubbles of air fizzing up through the water coalesced into a small spinning whirlpool again.

"I'd owe you one. Or two," I told it aloud.

With a bounce, the whirlpool zoomed toward Kalypso. It skirted close enough to Poseidon on its way to lift his toga, showing me the dark shorts I now knew he wore underneath, then smashed into Kalypso.

As it hit her, it expanded, lifting her high in the water and turning her over and over. Fortunately, she was wearing underwear too, as the skirt of her dark dress flipped up and I heard her give a roar of anger. The whirlpool grew again, then launched her bodily up through the surface of the water. A second later, far in the distance, I saw a disturbance in the water signaling her return to the water.

Poseidon turned slowly to me, and I snapped my hanging jaw closed.

I tried to look cool as Poseidon gazed at me, his eyes burning with blue light. Stone was creeping over his neck and up his jaw.

"That was impressive," he said carefully.

"Thanks." I looked at the whirlpool, still ten feet tall and churning near the surface. "And thank you!" I called to it. "You kicked that Titan's ass!"

With one last whizz, it dissipated.

"I suggest we swim in the opposite direction that she came back down in," Poseidon said.

"Lead the way, sire," I said, giving him a salute. A heady adrenaline was rushing through my body, a sense of surrealism taking over my rational thoughts.

I was in the goddess of love's lethal underwater garden, and I'd just used air magic to pitch a frigging Titan over a hundred feet.

How in the hell had I ended up here, all the way from the shitty little trailer in Oxford?

My sense of wonderment at my situation only increased as we continued to swim. The landscape beneath us changed again, the vicious pink weed petering out and replaced once more with bright green, bubbling grasses. But soon, there were also shoots. They started out quite small, maybe only a few feet. But the farther we got, the taller they grew, until they reached the surface of the water. We had moved away from the bowl, taking one of the tributaries that led off in the opposite direction as the now-probably-fuming Kalypso, and we had been swimming in a gentle bend, the bowl no longer visible behind us.

Soon, it was as though we were in an underwater forest, the colossal roots of the plants stretching up to the sun like tree-trunks around us.

They began to don canopies that looked like giant lily-pads above us, bright orange and purple, changing the color of the light seeping down through them and casting weird shadows over us as we moved.

I got the heightened sense of being in a dream, but I wasn't entirely sure it was a good one anymore. There was something both beautiful and eerie about the forest.

I slowed down as something alongside one of the tall roots caught my attention. It was a faceted column of some sort with a triangular top, sticking up out of the grassy riverbed. It was gray in color, and as I looked closer, I realized it was made from stone. As we neared it, an opening appeared in one side, small and dark.

Concern surged through me, the sense of danger arriving almost too late.

"Stop!"

Poseidon paused and turned to me just as something fired from the stone column, whizzing past his face by mere inches. If he hadn't turned, the thing would have hit him.

"What's wrong?"

"That thing just shot an arrow or something at you," I said, pointing to the column.

He turned, and I yelled again. "Move back!"

He did, but not before another arrow left the column, zooming toward him. He darted back out of its path. "I saw the arrow," he said slowly. "But not where it came from."

"That column."

"I do not see a column."

His gurgled voice was deadly serious, and I frowned.

"How can you not see it?"

"There is nothing there. Although I presume you speak the truth."

I snorted. "Why the hell would I lie?"

"My thoughts exactly. If there are sentinels, then we are likely on the right track to something worthwhile. Are there more?"

"Sentinels?" I asked, as I strained my eyes, trying to see further along the swaying tree-like roots. I caught a few glimpses of gray stone between the trunks.

"There are more. But if you can't see them, how are you going to carry on?"

He paused. "I can't. You will have to."

"Huh?"

"You can clearly handle yourself. You go. I will watch your back from here."

I swallowed hard, and Kryvo heated on my chest. "We can do this, right Kryvo?"

"No."

Lily's face filled my mind. *Of course you can. You just beat Kalypso.*

I screwed my face up. *Only because she was distracted by Poseidon and not expecting it.*

Nonsense.

"I'm not fast enough to get past the arrows," I said to Poseidon. "But you are. I think we have a better chance together."

It was true, I did think we had a better chance together. But I also really didn't want to carry on without him.

He regarded me a moment, silver hair floating behind him. "Agreed."

He held his hand out, and I took it. "Let's go low," I suggested, eyeing the height of the column.

As soon as Poseidon began to move lower, the stone column began to fire arrows. He was fast enough to duck under it, but when I looked left I realized we'd moved straight into the path of another, lower column.

"Go back up!"

He did.

I didn't dare to blink as we moved, swinging my head from left to right and shouting instructions as Poseidon kept us speeding through the gauntlet of arrows.

"Up!" I yelled, then, "Up again!" Arrows flew by, some a safe distance away and some so close I could feel the current they caused against my skin.

Poseidon kept zooming us forward until the thickening forest of roots and columns seemed to abruptly thin out, a large clearing coming into view.

"I think we're good," I gasped, as we burst into the clearing, scanning furiously for stone sentinels but seeing none.

"Thank fuck," Poseidon grunted, slowing us to a stop. His voice was strained.

"You okay?" I asked as I faced him.

He wasn't. I could see that immediately.

Blood streaked down his arm, and the stone was now covering more than half of the skin I could see.

"One hit me. I believe it is poisoned. I am weakening fast."

"Shit."

"We must find the red shell and leave here as soon as possible. I will need healing attention very soon."

"Shit, shit, shit."

Fear was working its way through me, and it wasn't just for losing him as an ally.

I was scared for him. The idea of him in pain, the tension in his voice, and the blood I could see — shining with silver as gods' blood did—was making me feel all kinds of wrong.

I needed him strong and healthy and... *happy*.

Why the hell did I need him happy?

Not the time, Almi. Lily's voice brought me out of my emotions.

"Not the time," I murmured.

Poseidon frowned at me. "The shell," he repeated, seriously. "I believe that may have something to do with it, given its color."

He pointed his uninjured arm at something enormous and red in the center of the clearing, and together, we swam toward it.

24

ALMI

The water seemed to heat as we got closer, and my brows rose as I took it in.

It was a flower of some sort, and it looked the tiniest bit familiar. It had a circular hole in the middle, the inside dark and foreboding, and was ringed with massive leaves that curled over the sides and were covered in bright orange dots.

"It's a corpse flower," said Kryvo.

"Corpse flower? Well, that doesn't sound good."

"If you take it out of the water, it smells like rotten flesh."

"Lovely."

"It's also toxic."

I could have guessed that from the brightness of its color. It was so red my eyes almost hurt to look at it.

"I'm going to go out on a limb and guess the shell is in that dangerous looking middle bit," I said.

Poseidon flicked a look at me. "Are you going to send your air magic in to check?"

"Sure," I shrugged, as my heart rate quickened. Having magic was cool as fuck, but I was going to try to act as mature about it as I could.

Air? Could you do me another favor?

The bubbles immediately formed the little whirlpool again, and it bobbed through the water to me.

"Thank you. Poseidon here is in a bit of a hurry, 'cos he got hit by a poisoned arrow, so if you could just dart into that massive flower over there and grab the shell for me, I'd be super grateful."

"I'd be even more grateful if you didn't harass me whilst doing so," Poseidon added.

A small smile sprang to my lips, and warmth flowed through my chest as I looked at him.

He was in pain, and our lives were very much at risk, yet I was pretty sure the so-serious-he-might-hurt-himself god had just made a joke.

The whirlpool zoomed to Poseidon, lifted his hair over his head in the water, bounced for a second, then zoomed over to the big red flower.

"I'll take that as a no," Poseidon sighed.

"Don't look at me," I said, holding up my hands. "I'm told you can't control air, only ask it for favors." I grinned at him, and he shook his head.

A noise made us both turn to the flower, high-pitched and quiet at first, then lower and more melodic.

"Is the flower… singing?"

My little whirlpool was lowering itself into the hole in the middle. As I watched, all of the leaves contracted suddenly, the hole closing, then bursting open again and shooting something into the water. It was a fine, shining dust, gold and red sparkling glitter shooting out for tens of feet in every direction.

Including ours.

"Kryvo, how toxic is this thing?" I asked him quickly, already moving backward.

"Extremely. You'll go mad, then you'll die."

"And how does it distribute its toxin?" I tried to keep the panic from my voice, but I couldn't see the whirlpool anymore, and the glittery stuff was falling fast through the water toward us. We were trapped in the clearing, the stone columns lining every exit I could see back into the forest.

"From what I can tell from this mural it, erm…" He trailed off and I swallowed.

"Shoots it into clearings where its prey is trapped?"

"Yes."

The water all around us rippled, and my head swam as glitter descended over my vision. The music got louder, an enchanting melody that seemed to build with each second. A calmness came over me, and the forest seemed brighter somehow.

Movement over my head caught my eye, and I saw giant red lily pads extending from the forest edge, starting to cover the clearing. The light changed color, reds and oranges stark against the green riverbed.

"It's so beautiful," I breathed.

"You're beautiful."

I looked at Poseidon, my breath catching at the look on his face.

Hunger.

Raw, unbridled, hunger.

The waves crashed over his toga, and he was a vision of strength and ferocity in the calm, beautiful, eerie underwater gardens.

The music built, and the more I stared into his face, the more I couldn't give a shit about anything but him.

Even the stone, edging his face and covering his arms, looked beautiful.

"Why are you so unhappy?" The question left my lips, and the words were instantly lost to the melody filling the water.

"You."

"I make you unhappy?"

"Every day."

Pain lanced through me, confusion stabbing at my consciousness.

"I don't want you to be unhappy."

Within a heartbeat, he was in front of me, one arm around my waist, the other pushed into my hair, drawing my face to his.

We turned in the water, my skirt flowing out around me as we spun, the world falling away, soft light, warm water, and delicious music engulfing me.

His lips were inches from mine, and I had never seen the waves in his eyes so clearly.

"You...I'm supposed to hate you."

Anger and fear pulsed across his features, the waves

roaring in the endless depths of his irises. "You will be the death of us both," he said, then his mouth met mine.

Desire exploded through me, my legs lifting, wrapping around him of their own accord. His tongue played across mine, then he was crushing me closer, kissing me like he had on the ship, like a man who would give up anything in the world for this taste. The taste of something forbidden, something worth risking everything for.

I kissed him back, with everything I could to match him. I had no idea a kiss could say so much, mean so much. But in that moment, I would have given up everything for him.

Everything?

The word repeated in my mind, quietly at first, then loudly.

Loudly, and in a voice that wasn't my own.

I froze, and Poseidon tensed. Our lips came apart, and I was suddenly aware that something was wrong.

The light had changed, darkened. The only thing now clear in the gloom was the corpse flower, glowing a rich red in the middle of the clearing. The lily pads above us had turned dark and opaque, and claustrophobia closed in on me.

Poseidon was still gripping me, my legs still wrapped around him, when a scream tore through the water. I tightened my grip as both of us snapped our heads round, looking for the source of the sound.

It changed, turning into a long, awful wail that made me feel sick to my stomach.

"What—?"I started to say, then I saw Poseidon's face. Horror was etched into his expression, and he pushed me away, blasting me back through the water. I tried to right myself, then stopped still. There was something in the water behind him. Lots of somethings. Wraith-like figures were swimming out of the corpse flower, glowing red, barely visible, and they were converging on Poseidon.

Fear so strong it was crippling my muscles expanded through me, my throat tightening and breath hard to get. The shrieking wail got louder, and my terror increased with it.

"Kryvo!" I half sobbed the starfish's name as Poseidon continued to stare at me in horror, the wraiths swimming around him. Each time they brushed his skin I saw lumps of his flesh fall away, turning to stone before they drifted to the bottom of the river.

"They're all dead," the starfish choked. His voice was tiny, and I tried to move, but my limbs were immobile. I was sinking through the water, unable to kick my legs to keep myself afloat.

Almi.

Lily's voice was crystal clear in my mind, and I sucked in a breath.

Almi, this is the flower's toxins. Swim to the flower, get the shell.

"I can't. Poseidon..."

He was being torn apart by the wraiths before me, and I couldn't do a thing. I was going to watch him die.

I couldn't. I couldn't see him die.

I needed him.

Almi, swim to the goddamn flower now!

My sister never yelled.

She never swore.

The shock leaked through my stupefaction.

"It's not real," I gasped.

It is not real. Kryvo said you would go mad, then die. Get to the damn shell.

"It's not real!" I repeated, loudly this time, yelling the words at Poseidon. "It's not real!" The third time saying it seemed to finally unlock my legs, and I kicked them hard. The wraiths all turned to me.

My stomach knotted itself completely in fear, and I almost locked up again, but Lily was there in my head.

Swim. You need to swim.

Gritting my teeth, I turned away from them, and swam for the flower.

25

ALMI

Tears streaked down my cheeks as I powered my way to the glowing flower. The closer I got, the louder the wailing scream got, so intense pain pounded through my head, and an overwhelming feeling of hopelessness seeped through me.

I forced myself on, through the barrier of awful sound around the corpse flower.

As I got over the top of it, my vision swam, everything wobbling and tipping from side to side.

Then the wraiths were *everywhere*.

They descended on me, smothering me with their translucent bodies, suffocating me.

"Swim down!" Kryvo's voice came to me, and I followed his instructions blindly, trying to angle my body down and kick my legs. I could feel my skirts getting stuck to my legs and anger began to replace my fear, frustration and terror bundling together, turning into something new.

"Keep going!"

My extended fingertips brushed against something, and a new vision filled my mind.

Lily.

On her pallet at Silos' home, the room burning around her. Flames licked at her bed, at her body, but they did her no damage. Because she was made completely of stone.

"No!"

"Almi, you're so close!" Kryvo's voice cut through the image, but when my own vision came back to me it was just the whirling bodies of the wraiths.

I kicked my legs hard and prayed.

Air! Help me!

With a blast of energy so strong I felt it to my core, the wraiths were thrown aside, leaving me a clear view straight down into the hole in the center of the plant. A solitary red shell was just within my grasp, and I lunged for it.

As I picked it up, another blast of the glittery stuff flew up around me, and a whirlpool as big as I was swept across me, picking me up and turning me face to face with Poseidon. Stone covered almost every inch of his skin, and I thrust the red shell toward him as black crept across the edges of my vision.

He wrapped his hand around mine, and everything vanished.

I found myself on a beach, white sand stretching in all directions. But I barely noticed it.

"Lily!" The image of the room burning around her stone body was seared into my skull, and the toxins still had me in their grip. Everything was spinning—the only thing keeping me upright was Poseidon.

We still had our hands gripped together around the shell, and when one of my legs gave out, he dropped to his knees with me.

"Almi," he murmured. "Almi."

I tried to focus on him, tried to see anything but the image of Lily.

His blue eyes bore through the flames in my head, and I clung to them.

"Poseidon."

He leaned forward, placing a kiss on my lips that was so tender it momentarily stilled my churning mind. "Almi," he murmured once more, then collapsed to the sand. I didn't have the strength to stop him pulling me down with him, and as I hit the ground, unconsciousness dragged me under.

When I awoke, all I could see was Lily. Flames were tearing down the room around her, and she lay lifeless, granite, in the center of the chaos.

"Lily!"

"It's okay, it's okay," a female voice soothed. "Lily's fine, it's a hallucination from the corpse flower's toxins."

I blinked up at Persephone's calm face. "What..." My words were cut off by a massive wave of nausea.

As if knowing, Persephone pressed a hand to my chest,

her golden vines flowing from her palm. The sickness vanished. "Good thing I'm good with plants," she smiled at me. "You should be dead."

"How's Poseidon?" I asked, taking a deep breath. "Where am I?"

"We're in your room."

"Kryvo!" Panicking, I pushed myself up.

I saw the starfish on the dresser, a paler red than he should have been. I struggled to get my legs out from under the covers, trying to get to him, but the sickness washed back over me, and I clamped my mouth shut and closed my eyes.

"Easy now." I felt myself pulled back to the bed, and my stomach settled again. "Is Kryvo your starfish?"

I nodded, unwilling to open my mouth in case I threw up.

"He's okay. Water creatures handle the toxins a bit differently. He'll need to sleep for quite a while, but he'll be fine."

Relief made me slump back into my pillows.

"As for your husband..." I sat up straight again, snapping my eyes open. "He's immortal, but the stone blight really has weakened him. He suffered from the poison in the arrow too, and it took a lot to get him conscious."

"But he's okay?"

"Yes." Her voice was uncertain, and I knew she wasn't telling me everything.

"What's wrong?"

"He is weak, Almi. So weak that I fear that overuse of his powers will render him a statue again."

"The blight is killing him," I whispered.

"Yes. I think so."

I bit down on my lip. "My power is finally showing up, I can communicate with air now. Does that mean the heart of the ocean will show up too?"

She shrugged. "Honestly, I don't know. Poseidon was the one who heard the prophecy from the Oracle, right?"

"Yes."

"Then you and he need to work this out. But I don't know you'll have much time before the next Trial. This is exactly what Atlas wants, each of you weaker every time."

I scowled. "Atlas is a cold, heartless asshole."

"Agreed. But he's not stupid. There is a ceremony in Aphrodite's palace tonight."

My stomach sank. "Shit. He's going to send us straight to the next Trial from there, isn't he."

"Probably. I should warn you, Aphrodite's palace is a little…tricky."

"Tricky?"

"I'll tell you when you've had some rest."

"Thank you. For saving us."

"You're welcome, Almi."

The next time I woke it was with the exact same image of Lily in the burning room filling my mind, swallowing me whole.

I heard myself scream as I thrashed out of the covers. "It was a dream," I panted aloud as the image faded and my room came into view.

"A bad dream."

My head jerked at the voice. "Poseidon!"

"Are you alright?" He looked concerned, his silver hair pushed back from his tanned face, his blue leather fighting clothes on. He was sitting in a chair that had been pulled up to my bedside and was leaning toward me.

"How long have you been here?"

"Not long. You were dreaming."

"Yes."

He gave me a long, intense look that never left my face. With sudden alarm, I looked down at myself. I was wearing a white shirt from the closet, I saw with relief.

Sending silent thanks to Persephone for dealing with my modesty while I'd been unconscious, I looked around the room. "Is there water anywhere? I'm thirsty."

He stood and moved to a tray on wheels that was covered in food and drink. "Persephone said not to eat too quickly, as it may make you sick," he said.

I nodded, eyeing him warily. "You are acting like my nurse." When his eyes met mine again, the memory of our kiss in the clearing crashed through my mind. I felt my cheeks heat.

"I felt the need to ensure your health," he said awkwardly.

"That, erm..." I took a quick breath. "That kiss. That was the flower toxins. Right?"

That didn't explain the kiss on the ship.

Or the way I felt every time my skin touched his.

Or my stupid burning desire for him to be happy.

"Right," he said. "Toxins."

"Toxins," I repeated, lifting a pastry covered in sugar from the tray, along with a glass of water.

He stepped back, putting some distance between us.

"Between toxins and marriage bonds, it's getting harder to hate you," I muttered around my pastry.

Emotion flashed in his eyes, and when he spoke his voice was soft. "You still hate me?"

I took a long swig of water from the glass, trying to work out how to answer him. My mind felt a little foggy still, but I was restless and painfully aware that I'd very nearly died. Deciding honesty couldn't hurt now, I replied as truthfully as I could.

"Yes. You took me from Lily. That was unforgivable."

"Unforgivable," he repeated quietly. "There is nothing that can not be forgiven." His eyes had turned hard, his jaw tight.

"I don't know if that is true."

"It must be," he said softly. "Forgiveness or revenge. They are all we have."

"What are you talking about?"

"Nothing." His eyes locked on mine. "What were you dreaming about?"

"Jeez, you're hard to keep up with, you know that?" I chewed on my pastry and glared at him.

"What do you mean?" He looked genuinely bewildered, and a modicum of pity worked its way through my annoyance.

"You say stuff, and I don't know what you're talking about. It's all mysterious, cryptic nonsense. Or you lose your shit and just leave halfway through the conversation.

You're not easy to be around." Not that that was stopping me wanting to be around him.

"I... am not used to sharing thoughts of this nature with others," he said eventually. "I suppose I am not very good at it." He said the words like they tasted bad, and I thought that he probably didn't admit to not being good at things very often. Or at all.

"You and Galatea talk about everything," I said, still chewing.

"Not things like this."

"Like what?"

He glared back at me, the waves growing in his eyes and his hands twitching by his sides. "Emotions," he spat, eventually.

I raised my eyebrows. "This is you talking about your emotions?"

He let out an angry sigh. "*You* do not make it easy."

"You don't deserve it easy."

I couldn't help being hard with him, I was battling a decade of anger. But the cold, hard, controlled sea god was trying to talk to me about emotions?

"Look, the only person I share stuff like this with is my imaginary projection of my sister. So, it's not like I'm an expert," I admitted. "But, I think we have to be honest with each other if we're going to survive this."

"There are things you can't know."

I sighed. "What a surprise. Will you tell me what you know about the heart of the ocean?"

"I already have. I know no more than you do now."

"Great." I bit off another piece of pastry as I rolled my eyes.

"What were you dreaming about?" The urgency of his tone made me look at him.

"My sister. The flower made me see her completely turned to stone, and the building she was in was on fire." I felt tears fill my eyes as I spoke, and I cursed them inwardly. I didn't want to look weak. "It was very vivid. And upsetting."

"The image is still clear to you?"

"Yes."

"When we were in the clearing I... I saw the water wraiths tearing you apart." Strain edged his every word.

"I saw that too. They were pulling off chunks of your flesh." I shuddered at the memory.

"But it is your sister you see in your nightmares?" he asked.

I stared at him as I nodded, trying to make sense of what he was implying. That my nightmares should be about him? Or that he was having nightmares about me? His gaze bore into mine, and then light flickered in his eyes.

"Would it make you feel better to see her?"

"What?" I scrambled to the edge of the bed. "What do you mean?"

"I will take you to her. Now. To put your mind at ease."

"You would do that?"

"Yes. You saved my life. Again."

I paused. "So, you'll take me because you owe me?" An unexpected stab of disappointment that he was only taking me out of obligation pricked at my excitement.

He opened his mouth to say something, then closed it, simply nodding at me instead.

"Fine. Leave the room so I can get dressed," I told him, swallowing down anything else I might have wanted to say. If he was really going to take me to see Lily, this was the wrong time to risk pissing him off enough to do his vanishing-in-a-temper act.

26

ALMI

I barely even noticed the clothes I pulled on from the closet. I couldn't think of anything I wanted more than to see Lily. To see that she wasn't turned to stone, and that the bakery wasn't burning around her. The image burst to life behind my eyelids every single time I closed them, even for a second.

My thoughts flashed to Poseidon as I hurriedly brushed my teeth. Was he seeing me torn apart by the wraiths every time he closed his eyes?

He was so damned hard to decipher. But I was growing certain that he cared about me.

I knew it must be the bond that was causing it, because I felt the same way. I was drawn to him, both physically, and in a deeper way - a way that meant his safety and happiness were not his problem alone any longer.

If that was how he felt about me, then I could deal with it. It was the marriage bond, and as annoying as it was, it was possibly the only thing keeping us both alive. Between his failing power and my growing magic, we had managed to survive three Trials now through combining our strengths.

Rushing from the bathroom, I moved to the dresser and peered closely at Kryvo. I couldn't see any movement, but when I hovered my fingers as close to him as I dared, I could feel a little bit of heat coming from his body. "Persephone said you were asleep, little buddy," I whispered to him. "I'm leaving for a short while, but I wanted you to know that you're safe here, and that you were frigging amazing. Sleep well, friend."

When I opened the door Poseidon was leaning against the frame, his stormy eyes conflicted and intense when they fell on me.

"Where are we going?" He held his hand out to me.

"Are you strong enough to flash us?" I wanted to get there as soon as possible, but I didn't want him to use power he couldn't afford to.

He scowled at me. "Flashing is child's play to a god," he growled.

"Fine. Fyka."

"That is your hometown."

"Yes," I nodded. "My friend has been taking care of Lily since you removed me from Aquarius." I glared at him, and he snatched my hand and flashed us out of the palace.

We were standing in the marketplace, and just about everybody within a hundred meters stopped what they were doing and stared. Poseidon wasn't known to be a hermit, but I didn't recall ever seeing the god in our little dome-town as a child.

I turned toward the bakery, and he followed me.

"Silos?" I called as I pushed the door open. It must have been around midday, because the place was packed with customers. A griffin spread his wings wide in surprise, hitting a merwoman in the face.

"He's out back," called a woman behind the counter, without looking up from wrapping a loaf of bread.

I pushed my way through the now silent group of people, to where I knew a section of the counter lifted to allow access to the back.

The matronly woman cast us a glance as we passed, and her mouth fell open as she did a double take. As one, most of the room dropped to one knee.

I shook my head as Poseidon inclined his at them.

"We know you're going to win the Trials, sire," a merman near the front said.

"Of course I am," Poseidon replied.

I rolled my eyes and kept moving.

"Silos?" I called again, once we were in the back part of the bakery, where both the ovens and the stairs were.

Just the fact that the building wasn't on fire was already making me feel better.

"Almi?"

A dark face emerged from a door, and Silos first grinned, then stared, as he saw Poseidon behind me.

He came out of the door fully and dropped to one knee. "You honor me and my bakery," he said.

"I'm here to see Lily," I said, and Silos lifted his head to look at me.

"Of course." I turned for the stairs, then paused when he spoke again. "I wasn't sure you'd made it," he said, his voice heavy with relief. I turned back to him, moving to give him a hug as he stood.

"I'm fine."

"Good."

When I turned back to the stairs, Poseidon was rigid. Ignoring him, I headed up the stairs.

I began to move quickly, the closer I got to her, and was practically running by the time I pushed open the door to her room. I rushed to her side, utter relief swamping me as I saw her flesh-colored skin. *Not stone.* Not the mother-of-pearl shine it should be either, but anything was better than stone. It had reached her shoulders, though, I saw as I pulled back the sheets.

I swallowed back the lump in my throat and sagged beside her. "Lily. Lily, I'm here," I muttered as I bent my head to hers.

A small noise reminded me that I wasn't alone, and I looked up to see Poseidon in the doorway. He was so large the room looked half the size, and all of a sudden, I didn't want him there. "You did this."

He shook his head gently. "I have made your life difficult," he said. "But I did not do this." He stepped further into the room, and I saw the stone spreading across his own flesh. "You can save her."

My heart almost stopped beating in my chest.

You can save her.

Nobody had ever said those words to me. Nobody other than me had ever believed them. A new hope coursed through me, as though the fact that somebody else believed the words might be true gave them actual possibility.

"I can save her?"

"You are the only person in Olympus who can save her. And me."

His words on the ship, when he had rescued me from the storm, rushed back to me.

"I will always save you."

And now… Now it was up to me?

I gripped Lily's cool hand, dragging my eyes from him to her. "How?" Tears streaked down my cheeks as I stared at her lifeless face.

"First, we rid this realm of Atlas. Then," he took a long breath, and I moved my gaze back to his. "Then, we do whatever it takes. The Oracle, Persephone's powers, even Atlantis if we have to. We go wherever we need to, do whatever is required to heal the families this blight has cursed."

More tears spilled from my eyes.

I wasn't alone anymore.

The commitment in his statement was the most sincere thing I had ever heard. He would not stop until we found a cure. And I knew it wasn't just to save his own skin. I knew it as surely as I knew my own name. The King of the Sea loved his people, loved his subjects.

"And the magical sleep?" I breathed.

"The Oracle will tell us more. She will be our first visit, when these cursed Trials are over."

I nodded, squeezing Lily's hand. "This will be over soon," I told her. "And I'll get to talk to you. For real. See you smile for real."

A sob broke my words, and my eyelids forced themselves closed as emotion overwhelmed me.

Warm arms wrapped around my shoulders as they heaved, and rather than pull away from him I found myself leaning into the god.

I hadn't wanted him to see me cry. Ever. Nor would I ever have expected him to comfort me if I did.

But he tightened his grip around me, and just held me, and my sobs came harder.

"I love her," I said, through my tears, the words lost to his chest as I turned into him. I didn't let go of her, or wrap my arms around him, I just pressed my face to his solid warmth.

"I know. We will help her. I promise."

27

POSEIDON

I thought I had felt my heart break a hundred times before, but watching her with her sister... Not from a distance, in secret, but close enough to see her hands shake, to hear every sob slice through me like a damned dagger to my heart — it was unbearable.

My control was becoming more tenuous every minute I spent in her presence. Watching the wraiths pull her body apart had almost broken me, and now the image was burned into my soul.

Never, ever would I let her be harmed.

"You did this."

That was what she had said.

She held me responsible for the pain and torment her loss caused her.

Every single part of me longed to be the opposite of that pain. To be the life, the healing joy, the freedom she so desperately craved.

But it was better this way.

I needed her to hate me.

28

ALMI

"I'm really starting to like these dresses," I told Kryvo.

"They are not practical for warfare," he said.

"No."

"Or hiding," he added.

"This is true. How are you feeling?"

He was glued to my collarbone, and Persephone had assured me that the miniature version of the vials Poseidon had been giving me to boost my strength would ensure he would be fine.

"A little tired," he said. "I am struggling to reach the starfish further out in the palace."

"You don't have to do this."

"I'm your friend."

"I know, and I don't want you to get hurt."

"You might need my help."

"You are very helpful," I conceded. "But we should be okay without you."

He heated on my skin, and when he replied, his tone

was loaded with indignation. "If you don't want me there, I shall not come."

"Kryvo," I said softly. "That's not what I meant. You got poisoned by a deadly flower like eight hours ago."

"So did you."

"Yes, and I would definitely take more time to recover if it was on offer."

"Humph."

I shook my head. There was a knock on the dressing room door, and Galatea entered.

"Blue suits you," she said when she saw me.

I was wearing a dress that could have come straight out of a princess movie, layers of tulle in shades of blue puffing out from my hips. The top half was essentially two long pieces of draped fabric that went all the way over my shoulders, waistband to waistband. I'd had Roz pin it across my chest so that any vigorous movement wouldn't expose my chest to the world. Kryvo sat a little further out on my shoulder than usual, to avoid being covered by the fabric.

My tattoo was visible between the edges of the deep neckline. The turquoise green had spread into a forest green, then a much paler shade. Almost half of the shell was in color now.

"Thank you," I said. "How are you?"

"I have been better. But I have made some progress on the palace infiltration." Her face tightened, a slight snarl appearing. "Snakes."

"Snakes?"

"Yes. There have been multiple sightings of golden

snakes in the palace, and I think they have something to do with Atlas."

"I thought I saw a snake at Apollo's courtyard," I said.

Her focus sharpened. "Where?"

"Near the merman who turned to stone."

Galatea clenched her fists. "I will catch one of those slithery bastards," she growled. "And find out how they are getting in."

I inched away from her. "You're aware that you're terrifying, yes?"

She looked at me. "As terrifying as you are odd?"

"Yup."

"I can deal with that." She gave me a rare smile.

"How long until this stupid ceremony?"

"Half an hour. Are you armed?"

I lifted my skirt to show her my dagger in my leg strap.

It was weird to think that when I'd started all this, the gadgets and gizmos in my belt had been the best hope I had. Now, the magic of air was on my side. No more water-root or stink bombs.

"That dagger is pathetic," Galatea said. She moved her arm, fishing for something on one of the many leather straps crossing her lithe frame. "Here."

She passed me a knife, eight inches in length but weighing hardly a thing. It had a thin symmetrical blade and a handle made from a shiny shell-like substance, with turtles carved into it.

"It's gorgeous," I said.

"And sharp. Be careful."

"Thank you."

"It's a loan," she said sharply.

"Of course."

She nodded, satisfied, as I slipped it into the leg strap, in place of my blunt dagger. "I hope you will not have need of it, though that seems unlikely." A dark expression took her face. "You got just two shells last time," she muttered.

"Did you see how many the others got?"

"No, all the flame dishes in the palace would only show you two. But I heard a rumor Ceto did well."

I frowned. "Ceto scares me."

"They should all scare you," Galatea said.

"Hello?" Persephone's voice called just before she stepped through the door. "Hey, nice dressing room. Not going to lie - I'm a little jealous," she said, looking around at the pretty room.

I beamed at her. "Hi. Please can you tell Kryvo it's okay if he's too tired to come with me tonight?"

She looked at the little starfish, then at me. "Honey, you need all the help you can get. I'm not going to tell him any such thing."

"Oh."

"I told you," Kryvo squeaked.

"Look, Almi, I just wanted to stop by to warn you about Aphrodite's realm."

Galatea's frown deepened. "I hate Pisces," she muttered.

I raised my eyebrows in apprehension. "Aphrodite is... away right now. It's a long story involving Ares that I'll tell you about sometime over wine. But right now, her son Eros is running things in her place. And he's just as powerful in the, erm, intimacy department, as his mom."

I blinked. "Intimacy?"

Persephone sighed. "The magic of love gods can have a powerful effect on people. Particularly Eros, who is a god of desire. The magic can make you..." she paused, casting about for the right word. "A lot more open to things that might normally make you uncomfortable."

I looked at her in alarm. "Are you talking about sex?" I hissed.

"Well, yeah. And when I first heard about it, I freaked out, thinking that the magic would make me do things against my will, so I wanted to tell you that is absolutely not the case."

I felt my shoulders drop a little in relief. "Oh thank god."

"Yeah, thank Athena and Artemis in particular, they're the ones who put strict rules in place about that sort of thing," Galatea said, pride in her tone.

"Because Zeus is a colossal prick," Persephone said. "Anyway, being in Pisces will only heighten your existing desires. You don't need to worry about doing anything you'll regret."

I swallowed. "What if I'm not sure about my desires?"

Persephone gave me a knowing look. "Then you might get sure, real quick."

29

ALMI

My breath stalled in my chest when Persephone flashed us to Aphrodite's realm.

Just like Apollo's party, we were where the Trial had just taken place. We were in a long rectangular space reminiscent of a temple, with regular columns holding up the ceiling, but three of the walls were missing. The floor led straight onto the sand at each end, and the river at the front, and it was made of glass, the view beneath us of the sandy shoreline dropping away and the vivid green underwater landscape we had been trapped in spreading out into the distance. A flashing image of flames and stone leaped into my mind, and I dragged my eyes away.

The back wall was covered in doors, each one a different shape and style. Heat rushed my cheeks as I scanned the paintings around the doors. All of them depicted couples in various states of undress or arousal.

I turned instead to the ceiling, inky blue and covered

in twinkling stars, in contrast to the warm sunset colors swathing the sky outside.

The area was packed with people, more than I'd seen at Apollo's or Poseidon's. Beautiful men and women roamed the room with trays of drinks, wearing barely any clothing. My cheeks burned even hotter as a topless woman with purple skin and flame-red hair approached us.

"Cocktails?" she beamed.

Persephone took something bright blue with an umbrella in it. "Thanks."

I did the same. Galatea shook her head tersely, making a point of not looking at the woman's chest.

"Try to have a good time here," Persephone said to me, lifting her glass to mine. "I don't want to sound all doom-and-gloom, but…" I watched her try to say what she was thinking, knowing exactly what it was.

"It might be my last chance to have fun?"

She gave my arm a gentle squeeze. "You never know what's around the corner," she said.

I did, though. I knew what was coming. Since giving in to my emotions so physically in Lily's room, I had never been surer of my immediate future.

We were going to hand Atlas his ass, then we were going to cure the blight turning the citizens of Aquarius to stone. Including the two people dominating my thoughts.

I looked over the guests and spotted Poseidon easily. He was talking with Athena, his back to me. But the second my gaze landed on him, I saw him tense.

"Excuse me," I said to Persephone and Galatea, and made my way over.

Nerves flitted through my stomach as I approached, both because I'd let Poseidon see so much of my emotion earlier, but also because he was with a freaking Olympian. One I admired.

"Athena," I said, bowing my head respectfully as I reached them.

She locked her eyes on me, and so did the huge owl on her shoulder. "Almi," she said. "You are doing well, for one so untrained." Her voice was deep and lyrical, and commanded instant respect.

"Thank you."

She nodded, looked at Poseidon pointedly, then turned away to talk to someone else.

"Why are you polite to her, and rude to me?" Poseidon said as soon as she was gone.

"Because she doesn't radiate go-fuck-yourself vibes all the time."

He frowned. "I beg to differ."

I laughed. "Fine, she does, but she doesn't do it in an arrogant way. She does it in a way that suggests she's earned it."

He stared at me a beat, then cast his eyes down my body so fast I might have missed it. "Your tattoo has more color."

"Yes. I hope that means I'm getting stronger."

"It is—" He clamped his mouth shut, as though he had been about to say something he shouldn't.

"It's what? What do you know about it?" I asked, stepping forward excitedly.

His eyes were bright with blue light. "It is beautiful."

"O-oh." Warmth flooded my chest, and the happiness those few words caused shocked me. "You think so?"

"Yes." The muscles in his neck were straining, and his chest was rising and falling too slowly, like he was breathing overly deeply.

"Thank you."

"I find many things of the ocean beautiful," he said, a forced flippancy to his tone. I might have been stung, except that the sincerity of his words didn't match the first sentence. He was covering up, pretending he hadn't meant what he'd said.

"So, you think we'll go straight to the next Trial from here?" I asked, changing the subject.

"It seems likely. Though Atlas is not here yet."

"Where is our host?" I asked, looking around the room. I had never seen Eros, also known in human myth as Cupid, before. He was rumored to be worth looking at.

Poseidon's face darkened. "Fortunately, not here. You should be warned that Aphrodite's bloodline, and her realm itself, can heighten some urges."

"Persephone has already briefed me," I said. "Do you know if my friend is here?"

Silos would bust something to be in a forbidden realm, especially with a bunch of topless women and sex paintings on the walls.

Shadows flashed across the light in Poseidon's eyes. "The baker?"

"Yes. Silos."

"Who is he to you?"

I jerked my head back, in both surprise and indignation at his forceful tone. "My friend. As previously stated, a number of times," I said, not trying to keep the defensiveness out of my tone.

"Is he aware that you are friends?"

"He's taken care of Lily for almost a decade; I don't think he would have done that if he wasn't my friend," I said, frowning.

"I meant, is he aware that you are no more than friends," he growled.

Anger coursed through me, replacing the warm feeling from before. "What the hell is that to you?"

He stepped closer to me. "We are wed."

I gaped at him. "Are you shitting me? You do not get to marry me, dump me in a different damn world for eight years, then claim me as your wife when it suits you!"

"Do you love him?"

The question was so abrupt, my tirade sputtered out completely. "Love him?" Poseidon just glared at me, his jaw so tight he may as well have been made from frigging stone again. "He's my friend! My best friend! What the hell is wrong with you?"

"You," he hissed.

"*I'm* what's wrong with you?" I said incredulously. "You need to take a look in the mirror buddy, because you are frigging nuts."

"So you do not love him?"

I shook my head, then downed most of my drink before I could lose my shit and throw it over him. "No, your watery lordship," I said, waving my hand at him angrily. "I love him as my friend and for what he has done for my family. Nothing more. Happy now?"

"No."

"What a fucking surprise." I finished the rest of the drink, barely noticing that it tasted like fresh strawberries.

"Have you lain with him?"

"Oh, for fucks sake." I turned, trying to flag down a server.

"Answer me."

"No." I swiped up a drink from a man wearing nothing but a piece of string masquerading as underwear.

"No, you will not answer me, or no you have not lain with him?"

"Jeez, I haven't *lain* with anyone, if you must know!"

Waves rushed his eyes, and he seemed to swell with power.

I gulped at my new drink, something watermelon flavored and particularly lovely. It did nothing to calm my burning face.

"I must leave."

"The party?"

"No. Your vicinity." With that he whirled away, leaving me staring at his back in disbelief.

"That man…" I fumed.

"God," Kryvo corrected me.

"God or not, he's a frigging nutcase."

"I think he finds you hard to be around."

"The feeling is mutual."

I heard a voice behind me, deep and powerful. "Whenever I see you, you are talking to yourself." I ground my teeth and closed my eyes. I *really* did not want to speak with the owner of that voice. I considered moving away, but my legs turned my body without me telling them to. I glared as I found myself face to face with Atlas.

30

ALMI

"What do you want?"

"I want you to know what kind of god your husband is."

"I don't care."

Atlas raised his eyebrows. "Am I supposed to believe you are in it for the power? The status? The world didn't even know who you were just a week ago. If you don't care about him, and you don't want to be a queen, what is it you want, little Almi?"

"What I want is none of your damn business, Atlas. Fuck off."

Anger darkened his face, flames roaring around him for a split second. The image of Lily burning flashed into my mind, and I must have reacted, because Atlas's gaze sharpened. "You are afraid of fire?"

"No."

"I could *make* you afraid of fire." His voice had dropped to a seductive, infinitely unsettling tone. Actual flames began to lick up around his toga-clad body.

"Leave me alone."

"No, I don't think I will. So far, you and Poseidon have felt little of the torment you both deserve. I need to up my game."

"You're insane. You know that?"

He laughed, the hint of mania I'd seen a few times in his eyes evident in the sound. "I am a Titan, Almi. Do you know what that means?"

"You're old."

"I'm more than old. I was here at the start. I am a part of the source of the very world you live in. Do you know what happens when a being this primordial, this *colossal*, experiences pain?"

I shook my head, unwilling to speak. He was advancing on me, the smell of electricity and fire rolling from him, the air thick.

"Love and loss. There's nothing more powerful. I will have my revenge, and there is nothing a pathetic little sea nymph and a broken, redundant Olympian can do to stop it."

I glared back at him, refusing to flinch, but desperate for him to leave.

"She told you to fuck off."

Poseidon's voice was loaded with power, and although I still couldn't turn around, I felt his presence behind me, and smelled the fresh scent of the ocean.

Atlas' unhinged gaze settled over my shoulder. "Are you enjoying the irony of your predicament?" he hissed.

I felt another wave of power wash over me, and the flames flickering over the Titan dulled. "You are responsible?"

"You must have guessed by now? Although, I suppose you are quite stupid."

"How long has it been since you were awoken?" Poseidon growled.

Atlas laughed. "I'm not wasting my time on you two, when there are so many more pleasant ways to pass moments in Aphrodite's realm. I think Kalypso is waiting for me, with a drink."

With one last craze-filled look, he strode away. My limbs loosened as he left, and I turned to Poseidon. He looked furious, and stone was spreading across his exposed skin.

"What was he talking about?"

"He is causing the stone blight."

"What?" I gaped at the sea god.

"I suspected he was, and it is important that it is confirmed. I must inform Galatea."

"So, that's why only Aquarius is suffering from the ailment? It's an attack on you."

"Yes. But my people are paying." Soft rage laced his bitter words.

"What did you do? Why did he say it was ironic?"

I didn't expect him to tell me, but when he looked into my eyes I didn't see the tight refusal that I had on previously asking about his feud with Atlas. Instead, more sadness filled the depths of his fierce blue eyes. "I do not want to tell you."

"Why not?"

"Many reasons."

"Are you... ashamed of what you did?" I barely whispered the words, somehow feeling like I was treading on thinner ice talking to him like this than when I yelled or swore at him.

"Yes. I do not regret my actions. But I do not wish to relive them. Or speak of them." He straightened as he spoke, his commanding presence growing, leaving no room to ask more.

I nodded. It was more than he had given me before, and he had been honest. That was enough. For today, at least.

"Do you, erm, want to dance?" The question left my lips of its own volition. A harp was playing, but there was a deep beat behind it, and it was penetrating my consciousness somehow, pulling me to it.

Poseidon looked at me, eyes sparking with light. "Music in the realm of love is a dangerous thing," he said, his voice husky. "It has a power of its own."

"I like it," I said.

"You're supposed to like it." He looked at me a second longer, before speaking again. "I need to talk to Galatea about the blight. I will return."

I watched him leave, wondering why the hell I'd asked him to dance.

I'd been mad at him getting all jealous about Silos literally less than ten minutes earlier.

You weren't really mad. Lily's voice popped into my head, her image floating swiftly into my mind. *You want him to be jealous.*

I sucked on my cocktail, refusing to answer. Mainly because she was right. Embarrassing as it was to admit to him that I was a virgin, there was a part of me that couldn't believe a god like Poseidon would give a shit about my relationship status. It was the same part of me that couldn't stomach the idea of him with someone else.

It's the marriage bond, I told Lily. *It must be.*

Yeah, sure. Nothing to do with the fact that he's seven solid feet of muscle, wrapped in the raw power of the ocean, and he looks at you like you're the only thing that could tip him over the edge.

I leaped on her words, ignoring the ones I didn't want to respond to. *Why is that? Why does he always act like he's about to lose control when he's around me? Maybe it's the stone illness, making him edgy.*

Lily laughed. *Dance with him. I think you'll work it out for yourself.*

I gulped more watermelon drink. *Work what out?*

The tension between you two. And don't worry, I will be making myself scarce, I promise.

Lily! As if anything like that would—

"Do you still want to dance?" Poseidon melted out of the crowd, hand held out toward me.

"I, erm, I'm—" All my confidence vanished.

"Technically, you are my queen. And I think it would be good to show Atlas some solidarity. It will anger him."

"Well. In the name of angering that jerk, let's dance," I said, steeling myself and taking his hand.

31

ALMI

We weren't the only ones on the dance floor. Couples were everywhere, many with their eyes closed, and a rhythmic sway to their movements as they pressed against one another.

"How can dancing to a harp be sexy?"

A few faces turned my way as I mumbled the words, drawn by Poseidon's presence. "This is the realm of love. Eros is here now." He pointed, and I saw a man standing at the edge of the room, framed by the water beyond.

Not just any man. He was ridiculously attractive, and not in a way that was dignified or regal, but in a way that made me think all sorts of things I usually only thought about when I was alone. He was broad and muscular, and wearing human clothes, tight pants and a shirt. His hair was dirty blond and I could see his bright blue eyes clearly as they fell on us.

"We must converse with him, as is polite." Poseidon's voice was sharp, and I wondered if there was something between the two gods as we made our way to the water's edge.

"Poseidon," Eros nodded as we reached him. "And Almi," he said, turning to me.

"Hello," I answered. I felt no waves of power like I did from the other Olympians, just a pleasant, relaxing sort of feeling.

"I'm sorry about my mom's sea garden trying to kill you," he smiled at me.

"I doubt that," Poseidon answered, before I could speak.

Eros looked slowly at him. "How is my mother?"

"Ask Hades."

"Sadly, he is engaged with Apollo, elsewhere, this evening." Eros' smile was still present, but there was a palpable tension between the two of them.

"Well, Aphrodite is in his care now."

A tense second or two passed, then Eros' full-lipped smile broadened, reaching his eyes. "You know, she can get a little crazy at times. Going after Ares like that…" He shrugged. "I'm sure a short spell in the Underworld won't do her any harm. And it's given me a chance to redecorate." He grinned as he nodded at the back wall.

"Very classy," Poseidon said, rolling his eyes.

Eros ignored him, looking to me instead. "Don't let this one fool you," he said. "This grumpy, stoic, boring vibe he puts out? It's all bullshit. I'm a god of desire, and let me tell you, this guy is fucking full to the brim with that shit. It's near killing him keeping it under control all the time."

I swallowed, my cheeks heating, as Eros' sparkling eyes bore into mine.

"Enough, Eros," Poseidon growled.

The god looked at Poseidon. "I'm just saying it how it is. If you don't let some of that shit out, it'll kill you. You'll explode."

"You are immature, and utterly unpracticed in self-control. I need no advice from you."

"Wrong. On a number of accounts. And anyway, who said I was talking about sex? Which, incidentally, there is nothing immature about."

The way he said the word sex made heat wash over me, leaving me even more flustered.

Poseidon growled his name in warning. "I said, enough."

"Desire is a broad word, Mr. Sea King. Deny yourself everything you want, and it won't just be your own life you ruin."

"I have had enough of your advice for one evening," Poseidon snapped suddenly.

Eros shrugged again, his smile still firmly in place. "Your funeral. Have a nice time, Almi. Make the most of the place."

He winked at me before he turned away, and I could have sworn the volume of the music increased, a new note on the harp setting my nerves tingling as the sensual beat pounded enticingly behind the melodic tune.

"He's got a point, you know."

"He's an idiot."

I turned to Poseidon, trying to tamper down the swirling heat wrapping around me, and my heightening senses. "I'm not talking about, you know, *sex*, either." I coughed awkwardly. "When we were in the stables, I could see how much you miss flying. You should let yourself do more things you want to."

The memory of that smile, only seen twice and seared into my damn brain, leaped to my mind. "You should smile more."

His hard gaze softened at my words, and emotion filled his eyes. "You speak of things you do not understand."

"Then make me understand."

I could see his indecision as he stared at me. "The prophecy," he said eventually.

"What about it?"

"You did not hear it all." Poseidon's chest lifted as he took a long breath. "The part you do not know is important. To both of us. I want to take you to the Oracle. I want you to hear the rest."

A fluttering in my stomach accompanied his words. I had spent years wondering about the prophecy, hating the Oracle for ruining mine and my sister's lives. The words of the prophecy came to me clearly.

'He who possesses the heart of a Nereid shall possess the Heart of the Ocean. True love is not a necessity, pure possession will seal the deal.'

But... there had been more. A part I had ignored, because it had no relevance to our situation at all, and because Poseidon had cut it off, mid-sentence. I struggled to remember it.

Something about true love not going unnoticed?

I needed to get to the sketchbook, check what had been said.

"Why can't you just tell me?" I asked Poseidon.

"Firstly, I am hopeful that it may have changed. Secondly, you will have a hundred more questions that I can't answer, but the Oracle might be able to."

"Do prophecies change?"

"Rarely. But sometimes."

"If it involves me, then I have a right to know. Just tell me."

"We can only win these Trials as a team, and I am not willing to jeopardize our lives, and the safety of my realm, with personal matters right now. We must wait until the Trials are over, and I have dealt with Atlas."

"Personal matters?" I muttered, glaring at him. "That's what you're calling this? Lily's life might depend on these *personal matters*. Hell, everyone affected by the blight could depend on them."

"If I don't win these Trials, they will no longer be my subjects to rescue."

The gravity of his words slowly sunk in. I remembered what Athena had said about how dangerous Atlas taking one of the twelve realms could be to Olympus, and how important it was that Poseidon win.

He was right. Atlas was the far more immediate danger.

"I am sorry."

I blinked in shock at his words. I had been about to agree with him, commit to winning the Trials. I had not expected an apology.

"For not telling me about the prophecy?"

He stepped close, startling me as he lifted my hand in his and pressed it to his hard chest. "Yes. For that. But I am also sorry for what I have done to you and your sister. I am sorry for the pain I have caused you. I am sorry for the time you have been alone."

"You are?"

"I am."

He bent his head, and brushed his lips against mine, the lightness clearly a request for permission.

"I thought you wanted to dance?" I whispered.

"I do not dance," he said. "I want to watch you dance."

"You do?" I asked, surprised.

"I do. Dance for me."

He pulled me into his arms, slipping one arm around my waist.

I didn't argue with him. I closed my eyes, and allowed myself to enter the music, the feel of his hands against my body, the scent of him around me, the electricity in the air all surrounding me, pulling me in and sweeping me away.

I let go, for the first time in what felt like forever, nothing hammering at my mind, compelling me to action. I was completely at peace, lost to the deep, sensual beat of the music. I was warm within the circle of his arms, and if he had ever been my enemy, I knew I now had nothing to fear.

I felt the light brush of his lips against my neck, the gentle brush of his breath against my ear. When my eyes flickered open, he was watching me, his eyes vibrant, powerful, and sparkling with blue fire.

Feeling bold, I placed both my hands on his chest, letting them run down his torso, over his impressive six-pack and back up to his shoulders. I arched my neck and kissed him, my tongue reaching out to taste his firm lips. He responded with a groan, his arms tightening around me and pulling me closer. His kiss deepened. I felt his hands slide over the bare skin of my back, down to my bottom, pulling me up against him. An ache rose within me, and I embraced it.

"Do you know where all those doors at the back of the room lead?" he growled against my mouth.

"No," I breathed back.

"They are magic. Private rooms for guests of Aphrodite who want to be alone. They give the occupant exactly what they want, when they want it." He moved his head back to gaze down into my face. Another request for permission, I realized, and nerves fired through me as I dazedly worked out what he was suggesting.

"I… I didn't know that," I said, trying to slow my racing heart, and building desire. "Like the Room of Requirement but for sex?" I made an awkward attempt at a joke, panic trickling through me along with pounding need.

"I have no idea what you are talking about, but I know what you require. Have you really, truly never been touched?" His voice was tense.

"Never."

"I will take my time. I will make your long wait worth every second."

32

ALMI

His mouth closed over mine again, and I clung to him, lost in the feel of his lips, his tongue, the way his body moved with mine. I heard the music change, but I didn't care. I wanted, needed, to be with him.

He took my hand in his and led me through the crowd of dancers gyrating to the new tune. Nobody so much as cast a glance at us.

"Choose a door."

Almost breathless with anticipation, I didn't even look at the decorations on them, just pushed the nearest one open.

I stepped into something that looked like it had been dreamed up in a Disney movie. A dirty Disney movie.

A huge, four-poster bed, with a canopy of soft drapes stood in the center of the room. The bedding was a rich navy blue, and the walls were adorned with more soft hanging fabric, in teals and turquoises. All of them were adorned with exquisite illustrations of couples pleasuring each other.

I turned back to Poseidon, and before I could say a thing, his huge hands gripped my hips and he lifted me from my feet, kicking the door closed behind him.

He set me down on the massive bed, kneeling between my parted legs, the skirt of my dress tangling between us.

A tiny voice pushed through my hazy desire. "Almi?"

Kryvo!

"Can you send my starfish back to my room please?" I whispered.

A smile pulled at the corner of Poseidon's mouth, and there was a tiny flash by my collar.

He leaned forward, kissing along my jaw, down my neck. "Do you know what I wanted to do when I saw you tonight?" he whispered, his voice husky with desire.

I shook my head.

"I wanted to lay you on a bed and do this," he growled, and then he pulled me to him, and kissed me once more. It was a possessive, demanding kiss, and my body responded to every move. I was lost in a sea of anticipation. I moaned as he pulled away again.

He moved back and undid the clasp on his toga. I watched as he did, mesmerized by his smooth skin, the play of muscles under his tanned flesh. He reached for me again, this time running his hands up my shins, slowly lifting the fabric of my skirts.

A tiny worm of fear worked through me at the foreign touch, and he paused. He lifted his hand to my jaw, stroking a thumb along my lip.

"I will just give you a taste of the pleasure you deserve. And only if you want it."

"We're not going to…" I fumbled for the right word, trying not to sound immature or stupid. "Go all the way?" I mumbled eventually.

He tensed, his bare chest heaving as he sucked in a breath. "I would do anything to claim you right here, right now, Almi," he growled. "But no. I just want to show you how good you can feel."

I tried to force out my desperation for him long enough to think rationally.

I wanted him. I knew that. And I trusted him. He wouldn't push me any further than I wanted to go.

I nodded. "Show me."

He pulled me even tighter against him, his fingers brushing against my skin as he kissed me deeply. I could feel his arousal hard against my stomach, and knowing he wanted me as much as I wanted him made even more desire fire through my body.

I moaned, wrapping my arms around him, but he pulled back, eyes burning blue.

Slowly, he lifted my skirts higher, exposing my panties. He didn't move any faster as he hooked his fingers into the waistband of my underwear. I lifted my hips to let him remove them.

A tidal wave of self-consciousness slammed into me as he stared at my nakedness - the only man who ever had. I instinctively brought my knees back together as far as I could with him kneeling between them.

His eyes locked on mine, wilder than I'd ever seen them.

"You are perfect. So perfect."

Some of the discomfort leaked away at his words. He touched my jaw once more, drawing my face to his, and I opened my legs again to let him lean into me, to plant soft kisses along my neck.

"So perfect."

The rest of my awkward fear vanished with each kiss, each careful caress of his hands.

He slipped his hand back to my knee, rubbing his thumb in slow circles but not moving any further up my leg. I whimpered and arched my back, needing more. His eyes cut to mine.

I reached forward, tentatively running my fingers down his chest, across his stomach and lower. He groaned as my fingers brushed against him, and a massive bolt of need stunned me as I realized how big he was.

How in the hell would that work?

Slowly, he lifted my hand away from him, and I reluctantly let him. "Let me concentrate on you," he growled.

There was something in his eyes that I didn't understand. Something reverent, almost.

I watched, breathless, as his hands slid up my thighs, then lifted my hips as he slid his fingers between my legs, kissing me again at the same time. His tongue probed, seeking entry. I opened my mouth, allowing him in and his tongue slid against mine at the same time he ran one finger along my wetness.

He spoke against my lips, his tone coarse, heavy with need that my entire body was mirroring. "I want you to feel good." His finger stroked along me again, and I gasped. "I want to touch you until you can barely breathe."

He began to rub small circles over me, concentrated on my clitoris, and it felt nothing like it had when I had tried on my own,

"Oh my god." My words were lost to his mouth, and I bucked against his hand, wanting more pressure.

But instead, he stopped, dipping his fingers to my entrance. I felt myself tense, and he paused.

"Do you trust me?" His finger flicked against me, gentle and exquisite.

I nodded. "Yes."

He pressed one finger into me, and my head tipped back, my eyes closing. I could feel the intensity of his stare, but all I could focus on was the unexpected, unfamiliar pleasure of his touch.

My stomach muscles contracted as he moved his finger inside me, stroking, exploring, and a long moan escaped my mouth as he pulled it out slowly, only to slide back in again with a second.

A slight bite of pain emanated from my core, but it faded in an instant, replaced by a pressure that I could barely tolerate, yet never wanted to end.

His thumb moved, and the gentle pressure on my clitoris returned. Another, louder moan sounded from my throat, and I heard him growl.

"Look at me."

I opened my eyes, lifting my head and staring into his burning eyes. I was trembling, my body tensing against the incredible feeling of his touch. He leaned closer, scratching his teeth along my throat, his fingers moving faster inside me. The pressure built as he watched my face, and he spoke again, the strain in his voice palpable.

"I want your first orgasm to be something you'll never forget."

A thousand butterflies took flight in my stomach, and I forgot to breathe as the pressure built into something I could no longer contain. Before I knew what was happening, a sense of falling and a flash of heat had me crying out. My hands gripped his shoulders as my head fell back, and my entire body convulsed with pleasure, every nerve ending on fire.

I lurched forward, pressing my face against his neck, whimpering as my orgasm poured through me, obliterating every other emotion.

"That's it," he growled, his lips moving along my jaw. "Let go."

And I did. My vision came in and out of focus as I came down from the eruption of pleasure, and I realized with a jolt of embarrassment that I was mumbling his name. He kissed along my throat, across my collar and my chest, back up to my lips, fingers stroking gently across me, playing, teasing me back to reality.

Then his kisses moved, and I sat up sharply, my eyes flying open as I felt his lips on my inner thigh.

"What are--"

"Lie back. This time, when you come, I want to hear my name. Loudly."

I moaned, my chest tight, and dropped my head back onto the pillow as his tongue and lips moved to my other thigh.

The pressure was building again already, and I could

feel him watching me as his lips and tongue moved along my skin, closer, closer to my aching center. Just when I thought I couldn't take any more of the need, his tongue flicked over me and my nerves were so raw that a bolt of sensation shot straight up my spine. I jerked under him, and his hands clamped over my hips, holding me still.

"Fuck, you taste divine."

I answered him with a moan. His tongue moved, swirling, gently at first, then harder as I pressed myself against him. I felt his finger, stroking along me, then slowly sliding inside me.

"Oh fuck," I gasped, as raw pleasure exploded through me. But before it could take me over completely, he withdrew his fingers, and the pressure of his tongue lessened to a tickle.

"Not yet, my queen."

My senses all fuzzed together.

"Please," I gasped, scrambling to my elbows so that I could look into his face.

He was beautiful. Hard and powerful and fierce and wild. I would be his if he asked me. At that moment, I would do any single thing he asked of me.

My emotions must have been clear on my face, because dark, wild desire flashed in his eyes, and then his mouth closed over me, his fingers working their blissful magic once more. I dropped back onto the pillows and allowed his hands and his mouth and his tongue and the fire in his eyes to take charge of my body.

He took me to the edge three more times, and each time, he pulled back and kept me from letting go completely. His breath was hot against my core, his fingers moving with agonizing slowness as I writhed, begging. I felt like I was burning up, every single cell crying out for his touch.

I didn't know how much more I could take, but I never wanted it to end.

"Now."

He growled one word against me, and it was enough.

My back arched and I came, but instead of the freefall it had been the last time, I was thrown into a maelstrom of pleasure. My core pulsed, my skin prickling and my toes curling as I cried out his name, wave after wave of release crashing over me.

"Yes," he growled, his fingers inside me, his tongue on my clit. "That's it."

He kept going until I was shaking, my body near collapse, my entire mind consumed by the pleasure his hands and his mouth were delivering. Only when the last tremors had faded did he ease back, planting soft kisses along my thighs.

I sucked in air, trembling. When my eyes cleared and I could focus again, he was standing, watching me. His erection was obvious under his toga, and it sent fresh waves of need pounding through me. What would it feel like, for him to slide that inside me instead of his fingers?

My core pulsed at the thought, and I sat up, pushing my hair from my face. "I want you," I said, my own voice hoarse.

His hands clenched at his sides, power bright in his eyes. "No."

"But—"

He cut me off, his voice louder than it needed to be.

"Almi, I am begging you. Do you have any idea how much I want you? To feel you around my cock, to fuck you until you scream my name over and over?" He ground his teeth as my eyes widened. "No, you must stop." Waves rolled in his eyes, his jaw tense.

I stared at him a moment longer, trying to wrestle my feelings under control.

I wanted him so badly it hurt. And I could see and hear how much he wanted it too.

If he didn't want to do this today, here, then he must have his reasons. And honestly, I could understand. When I forced myself to think rationally through my heady desires, this wasn't the place I wanted to lose my virginity either.

I had no doubt in my mind that it was with him that I would do so though. I was connected to him far more deeply than I could ever have guessed. His expertise went farther than clever fingers or tongue. It was as though he'd known me, known my body, known my limits.

"Then kiss me," I said.

Some of the tension relaxed in his shoulders, his eyes softening. He moved back to the bed, and I arranged my skirt across my legs, trying to prove to him that I wasn't going to try to mount him. Though it took more willpower than I knew I had when he did sit beside me, cock clear through the fabric of his toga, not to climb into his lap.

I bit my lip as my eyes snagged on it, then dragged them to his face. "That was… amazing."

"I didn't hurt you?"

I shook my head. "Not a bit."

"I will never hurt you. I meant what I said before. I will always save you. Always."

I wanted to ask him why. I wanted to understand how he could feel so intensely for a woman he had ignored his whole life. But instead, I found myself leaning forward and touching my lips to his, pushing my hand into his hair, and pulling him close to me.

"And I you," I said, the words coming instinctively.

A gong sounded, and pain pierced my skull, sharp and startling and so unlike the explosion of pleasure I had just experienced.

"It is time to count the shells!" There was a harsh flash of red light, and suddenly I was standing in the main room again. My skin burned as I felt about myself, making sure my skirts were straight and trying not to look like we'd been up to exactly what we *had* been up to — although I was probably of the least interest in the room. Some unfortunate folk had clearly been enjoying the palace's atmosphere a little more... *unclothed* than I had been. I tried not to look, as humans and creatures alike scrabbled to arrange themselves more modestly.

Poseidon was beside me, and he gripped my hand, glaring at Atlas. The Titan was leaning against a column, smiling unsettlingly at everyone. Kalypso was a few feet from him, Polybotes towered over everybody in the room on my left, and Ceto was at the front of the group, everyone giving her a wide berth.

"Hey, the pleasure rooms in this realm are completely private, you can't just summon people out of them!" Eros came stamping through the crowd, his gorgeous smile conspicuously absent.

"I think you'll find I can," Atlas said. "Your pathetic Olympian magic is no match for my Titan power, as I just demonstrated."

Anger and a teeny hint of fear worked its way through me. Atlas *was* strong. He had infiltrated Poseidon's palace, and so far, little seemed beyond his capability.

"You will not be welcome here again." Eros folded his arms across his toga-clad chest.

"I weep for my loss," Atlas said sarcastically. "I'm sure your mother will beg to have me in her palace when the Poseidon Trials are over. In fact, I'm sure your mother will beg to have me, period."

Atlas' manic smile was back, and power burst from Eros as massive white wings erupted from his back.

Athena and Poseidon stepped forward together, along with the Hawaiian-shirt-wearing Dionysus and a man with short red hair, who I was sure was Hermes.

"Atlas, we agreed to these Trials and nothing more. Please conduct them presently." Athena's lyrical, deep voice was so formal she reminded me of a schoolteacher. "Eros, we will be leaving your realm imminently, please step back." She oozed command, and I wasn't surprised when Eros did as she asked him. He kept his furious glare trained on Atlas though.

"As you wish, mighty Athena," Atlas said with a mock bow. He waved his hand as he straightened, and the flame dish appeared, showing the vases full of shells. "Kalypso found two shells, bringing her score to nine." The beautiful water goddess scowled. "Now, after finding three shells, Ceto is at ten." The mother of sea monsters squelched on the glass floor as her vase filled higher. "Polybotes got two shells, making his total five." Atlas fixed his eyes on me. "Which means that with her two shells, Almi is just ahead of him, at six."

"No." I shook my head hard. "I got no shells in the last Trial, they were Poseidon's."

"No, I was watching. I saw you get both of them."

"Last time you said it was who was holding them when the Trial ended!"

He shrugged. "I changed my mind."

Fury coursed through me, but when Poseidon squeezed my hand and I looked at him, I didn't see my anger reflected in his face.

"We will talk alone," he said, so quietly I was pretty sure only I heard him.

"So, that means Poseidon still has zero shells!" Atlas announced, holding his arms up. "The mighty King of the Sea, and he can't win one solitary shell." He tutted, shaking his head. "Time for another go, I think."

With a flash, the room vanished.

33

ALMI

I wasn't surprised when I found myself in water, but I was surprised by how dark it was. I thrashed around in a panic, trying to get my bearings, and sending a silent plea for the breathing bubbles.

I felt them before I saw them, rushing around my face, cool compared to the water. Tentatively I parted my lips. Air, not water flowed between them.

"Thanks, air," I said gratefully, slowing my movements and trying to see what was around me.

The only light was not coming from above me, but below me, which had caused my disorientation. It was coming from a river of glowing lava, hot jets of water shooting up from the cracks in the black rock of the ground. As my eyes adjusted to the gloom, I started to pick out details, though I was unable to see Poseidon.

The landscape was like something from a nightmare, where hell met the bottom of the ocean.

A faint glow caught my eye and I tensed, until I realized it wasn't red, like the lava or the rotbloods. It was blue.

Poseidon, I saw with relief. He moved through the water with no resistance at all, reaching me fast.

"Are you okay?" his gurgled voice asked.

"Yes. But— I don't have Kryvo."

The realization smacked into me.

"He's safe," Poseidon said, taking my hand. "We must hurry. We have to find as many shells as we can."

"What's the point? He just gives them to me anyway."

"Which is a good thing. If they were split between us, neither of us would have a chance of beating Ceto or Kalypso by now."

He was right, I realized, as my brain caught up. "Ha!"

A tiny smile pulled at Poseidon's lips in the darkness. "He has shot himself in the foot, trying to humiliate me. Come."

We swam through the water, the river of lava beneath us widening, the speed of the sludgy orange liquid picking up as we moved along it. Something flickered with light, and I tugged on Poseidon's hand as I twisted to look. He stopped instantly, and I let go of him and turned to what had caught my attention.

It was a giant clam shell by the side of the river of lava, closed but pulsing with a very faint blue light.

Poseidon zoomed down toward it, and I followed him, swimming fast but not so fast I would tire myself out. By the time I reached him he was trying to prize open the huge shell with his hands. It was as wide as I was tall, the back half of it fused to the rocky ground. The water was hot so close to the lava.

Poseidon lifted his arm over his shoulder and slid his dagger out of the back of his ocean-toga. With an obvious effort, he wedged the tip of the blade into the clam. Slowly, the shell began to creak open.

I barely kept back a scream as the clam sprang open suddenly, spewing forth hundreds of tiny snakes. All of them were burning red or orange, looking as though they were made from the lava itself. They wiggled through the water at speed in every direction, and before I could do a thing, a handful of the foot-long snakes had reached me. They whipped me with their tails as they surrounded me, leaving searing hot pain where they touched my skin. I yanked the blade Galatea had loaned me from my leg strap and swiped at a snake that had just whipped its tail across the top of my arm. It hissed as I made contact.

I heard a distant growling sound and looked back at the clam. Poseidon was hacking away at a mass of the little snakes in the very middle of the now open shell, trying to get them away from whatever it was they were protecting in the middle.

"Air, if you could help out right now, I'd sure be grateful!"

Pain shot through my wrist, and I beat at the snake that was trying to wind itself around my arm. Blisters were popping up on my skin where they'd touched me, and I gritted my teeth and brandished my blade at the bright, burning serpents.

Another roar reached me through the water, and an explosion of the lava snakes blasted away from Poseidon, revealing a black chest the size of a jewelry box. He tipped forward in the water, snapping the lid open fast and swiping up a tiny, gleaming, white shell. He whizzed through the water toward me, grabbed my wrist and pulled me away from the snakes. I winced as his hands touched the blistered skin on my arm, and his head snapped round to mine.

Anger flashed in his bright eyes as he saw the evidence of the little lava serpents.

"One shell down," I said, as cheerfully as I could.

He slowed a little, having put some distance between us and the snakes, then passed me the shell. I took it, inserting it carefully into my bra, and he gestured for us to keep moving.

It was so dark it would have been easy to get lost, and I was glad when Poseidon began following the glowing river again.

An eerie orange glow fell over the black rock as more and more of the ground was covered in the surging molten red liquid. Just a moment later, the ground beneath us fell away, and the river of lava turned into a frigging *waterfall* of lava.

It was as beautiful as it was terrifying, streams of bright red and orange crashing over the edge of the rocky cliff into a massive pool far below us. Poseidon tilted his body in the water and headed down, keeping us a fair distance from the lavafall.

I could see movement in the lava as it fell, as though life churned inside it. I was just thinking how unnatural the whole thing felt, when a rotblood materialized from the falling lava. The inky red, blood-like liquid that the creature was made from swirled in tendrils out of the lava and solidified into the shark-shaped monster, and its huge mouth opened, rows and rows of sharp teeth visible as it sped through the water.

34

ALMI

Fear gripped me, but as I began to react I realized it wasn't swimming toward us. Poseidon slowed, jerked us back and stopped, then pointed.

Ceto.

The goddess was deeper than us, down by the huge pool, and she was trying to fish something out of the lava with a long, jagged bit of rock. The rotblood was heading straight for her.

At the last moment, she looked up and saw the demon shark creature. I expected her to swim away, but all she did was flick one of her tentacles, her expression barely even changing. Bright red liquid oozed from the tentacle, clouding around the rotblood. It jerked in the water, coming to a complete stop just a few feet over her head. With one final convulsion, it floated down the rocks beside her, unmoving.

"I do not want to be poisoned again."

Poseidon looked at me. "We will go back the way we came."

But no sooner had we started to turn, when a cackling sound reached me, followed by a blast of warm water.

We both whirled back to see Ceto rising in the water, red eyes fixed on us.

"Air!" Poseidon gave my hand a hard squeeze, before letting go of it. I was both touched and alarmed he appeared to think I could handle myself.

Three of Ceto's tentacles wriggled before us, her skin rippling just like the rotbloods. Liquid poured from the three tentacles, red, green, and black in color. Poseidon held up his hand, and a ribbon of water shot from his palm, expanding into a wall as it moved toward her.

A small change in the movement of the water around me suddenly turned into a large change, and a ribbon of air appeared in front of me, tightening into the little whirlpool.

"Hey!" I said, delightedly. "Help get rid of the poison!"

The little whirlpool whizzed off, spinning around Poseidon enough to lift his toga, before charging toward his wall of water. The second the two met, a blast of energy rolled through me, starting at the top of my head, and flowing deliciously through my whole body. My skin tingled, and all I could think about was him. When I locked my eyes on his face, he turned, and I knew without question that he could feel it too. A new light shone in his eyes, not the usual, piercing blue, but a blue so pale it was almost silver.

A loud hiss made us both look back, where our hybrid whirlpool had smashed into Ceto. It was ten feet high, glowing blue water spinning with the air magic, which also had a faint silver glow. Was that what I had seen in Poseidon's eyes just then? A reflection of my air magic when the two had met?

Colored inks flew from Ceto's tentacles as she struggled. She was getting free.

"I know you've got your hands full and all, but if you get a chance, see if she has any shells on her," I told the air.

My mouth fell open as the whirlpool abruptly tipped, turning Ceto completely upside-down. The goddess made an awful grating, growling sound that set my teeth on edge, then a huge swell of dark water began to form around her.

A sense of danger seeped through me, feeling her magic build. Poseidon grabbed for my hand. "Time to go."

"Wait! We can beat her."

Poseidon raised an eyebrow, and I saw the stone edging his jaw.

But he nodded. "On the count of three, we send her flying, just like Kalypso."

"Might have to be a count of one," I said, as I turned back to her. She was surrounded by a swirling black mass of red-veined lava, our whirlpool significantly slower around her, as though it were struggling to contain her.

"Now!"

I threw as much mental command as I could into my plea as Poseidon held up both his hands. "Send her as far from here as you can!"

The whirlpool glowed silver and blue, so bright I had to shield my eyes. Ceto hissed again, and then the whole thing rose through the water, taking her with it as it got high above the lavafall crater. The spinning got faster, and then Ceto burst out of the side of the whirlpool, her slimy body flying through the water, quickly lost to the gloom.

"Fuck! Did you see that?" I turned to Poseidon, unable to keep my excitement hidden. His eyes were still alive with glowing energy when they met mine. Surprising me, he moved forward, planting a brief but fierce kiss on my lips.

When he pulled away I moved with him, wanting more, but my little whirlpool forced its way between us, dancing through the gloomy water. There, in the middle of the swirling air and illuminated by its faint silver glow, was a shell.

"You little thief!" I exclaimed. "You actually managed to steal one of her shells? You're so clever!"

The whirlpool soared up and around us, lifting Poseidon's toga once again as it went, and I laughed as he scowled at it.

"We must move on. Without your emotional support starfish, we do not know how much time we have left." He reached for my hand as I felt a pang of unease at not having Kryvo with me.

"Yes. More shells."

We moved back into the lavafall crater, where there was a series of small, interconnected pools of lava, the ooze dripping from one into the other over the gentle slope. Poseidon headed straight for where Ceto had been, and I saw a small wooden chest sitting on a little island in one of the pools. My little whirlpool had accompanied us, flitting around us like it was on a serious caffeine rush, never staying still for a second. Not that I minded. I was quite happy to have air with me.

"Can you get the chest?" I asked it.

It zoomed toward the middle of the lava pool, and as it spun around the box, the lid flipped open. Poseidon swam higher so that we could see into it, but there was no shell. There was a small piece of paper.

My whirlpool shrunk, so that it was only six inches tall, and dipped into the chest. When it rose, the paper was in its center, and it whizzed back to me.

I unfolded the paper, and Poseidon moved closer to see. There was a crude drawing of a curved shape, and a dotted line crossing it, with an X at the end.

"I think it means under the lavafall."

"What? As in, go through the frigging lava?"

"Yes. It would be challenging enough for a deadly trial."

I looked nervously at the torrent of lava plunging over the drop-off and into the pool below. "The same lavafall that burps out demon sharks?"

"Yes. The very same."

"We need to do what we did before. Combine the water with your air," Poseidon said.

I nodded. "To make a clearing through the lava?"

"Exactly."

"You up for that?" I asked my whirlpool. It bounced in

the water, then expanded suddenly, making itself the same size as me.

Poseidon lifted his hand, ribbons of water flowing from his palm. Almost majestically, they threaded themselves into the whirlpool, beams of shining light spinning before us. I felt the same bolt of energy take over my body, the heady, intoxicating feeling filling me from head to toe.

The whirlpool moved, tipping and narrowing so that it became a horizontal tube. With a flourish, it powered toward the lava fall, stopping in the center. The lava flowed over each side of it, a perfect tunnel created through the sheet of molten liquid. I started to celebrate, turning to Poseidon, but a dull pain entered my head, seeping through me. The top of the tunnel dipped, and Poseidon squeezed my hand.

"Focus. We must go now. Do not lose concentration."

I did as he said, pouring all my thoughts into the whirlpool.

Keep the tunnel open and steady. You can do it, I thought, as I got closer. Heat overwhelmed me, and the tunnel side vanished, allowing lava to pour down exactly where we would be if we were inside.

"Focus!"

The heat won't kill you, Lily's voice said in my mind. *Concentrate on the air. Feel it. Imagine standing on the deck of that Crosswind, the wind whipping around you, taking you anywhere you want to go. Feel the wind.*

I did as she said, not risking closing my eyes, but trying to transport all my other senses just as she had described.

"We'll go one at a time. You first."

Poseidon let go of my hand, and with a deep breath and a sick feeling in my stomach, I swam through the air tunnel.

I was through in less than a second, but it felt like an age. I didn't stop to take in my new surroundings, just whirled around to see Poseidon coming through safely. As soon as he was by my side the whirlpool squished to nothing, the pain leeching through me vanishing.

"Air? Are you okay?"

There was movement on the now complete curtain of lava right in front of us, and I held my breath, terrified of a rotblood bursting forth.

But it was my little whirlpool that emerged. It spun fast, tiny droplets of lava soaring from it, almost like a dog shaking itself.

"You did good," I told it. To my surprise, it moved to Poseidon, nudging at his palms.

"I think it likes your water," I said.

"They are a good team." His eyes fixed on mine, and I knew he wasn't just talking about the magic.

A cracking sound forced us to look away from each other.

The cliff behind us was lit clearly by the lavafall that we were now behind, and the rock was shifting, creaking and cracking as we watched. It didn't look like it was in imminent danger of collapsing, more that it had its own life.

Poseidon took my hand, and we headed deeper, sticking close to the wall. It wasn't long before we came across a very wide, shallow cave.

· · ·

Keeping my eyes wide open in preparation for rotbloods, I scanned the cave. It was lit by an orange glow coming from the cracks in the black rock at the back. We swam cautiously along the length of the cave, and I wished Kryvo was there to tell us how much time we had. And to distract me from my growing unease.

"There," I said, pointing.

There was a stone statue, standing in the cave a little further along. We swam toward it, and I couldn't help my curiosity as its details became clear.

It was clearly very old, the stone chipped and worn. It was of a woman, very beautiful, wearing a toga and an extravagant crown. But rather than sit on hair, the crown was wrapped around a nest of snakes. There must have been a dozen making up her hair, and the detail in their faces was exquisite.

Poseidon jerked to a stop as we got within a few feet.

"She's beautiful," I said.

"We need to find the shell." His clipped tone made me remember the time pressure we were under, and I nodded.

I became aware of movement in my peripheral vision, and turned my head, hoping it was my whirlpool.

It wasn't. The glowing red swirls of a rotblood were growing clearer as it moved through the cave toward us.

Poseidon pulled my hand, making me look the other way. Another rotblood.

"Quickly."

I swam to the statue, looking carefully at the snakes first, as they drew the most attention.

When I reached forward to touch it though, Poseidon

slapped my hands away, pressing his own fingertips to the stone before I could object. I frowned at first the tension on his face, then the relief when nothing happened.

"It may have been a trap. Come on, help me search."

I nodded. "Air, can you hold off the rotbloods for a few minutes?" When I turned to locate the whirlpool, my stomach clenched. There were at least five more demon sharks closing in.

The whirlpool expanded, zooming protectively around us and the statue. "Thank you," I whispered, then turned back to the statue. Poseidon was running his hands over the snakes, so I dipped in the water, inspecting the rest of the carving.

She was wearing a belt, I saw, and in the center was an emblem so worn I couldn't make it out. It was orb-like in shape, and I ran my fingers around it, trying to see if it would reveal anything not immediately obvious.

I tugged a little too hard, and the orb came off in my hand. "Shit," I muttered, turning it over. There was a tiny hole in the back. "Poseidon!"

He turned to me and I held it up. A ribbon of water left his fingertip, and narrowed into a tiny point, slipping into the pinprick hole.

Red light flashed to my side, and I glanced sideways to see my whirlpool ram into a rotblood, sending it powering backward, before zooming to my other side to deal with another one.

I felt a pop, and looked back at the stone orb in my hand. It had opened a crack. I tried to open it the rest of the way, but it wouldn't budge. I could just make out something written in the ancient language on the inside lip of the opening though. I held it up to Poseidon, trying to ignore the barrage of gnashing teeth trying to get past my whirlpool to get to us.

"What does it say?"

I could have sworn I saw a flicker of fear in his eyes, before he spoke one word. "Ekdíkisi."

The orb snapped open all the way, revealing a tiny red shell in its center. I reached for it, and everything went dark.

35

ALMI

The palace courtyard materialized around me, and I blinked around in stunned triumph. We had done it. My *magic* had done it. It had helped us beat Ceto, survive the tests and traps, and even better – get shells.

"Three shells!" I turned, clutching at Poseidon's arm, and stilled at the wildness in his eyes as I made contact with him.

Freedom.

The feeling powered through me, so strong, so overwhelming, that everything else faded away but the promise in his eyes.

A life spent soaring through the sky, blasting through the waves, sea, wind and endless, boundless time and space—

"Almi." My name on Poseidon's lips cut off the stream of vivid thoughts, and without hesitation I lifted myself onto my tiptoes and crushed my lips to his.

I gave no thought to the folk around us, or the fact that we might be being broadcast. And nor did he.

He returned my passion with an unrivaled intensity of his own, wrapping his powerful arm around me and pulling me tight against him. Tight enough that I could feel how much he wanted me.

His tongue found mine, and desire coursed through my whole body, hot and almost painful in its urgency.

"Sire!" Galatea's shrill voice forced us apart, and I panted slightly as I turned to his first-in-command, trying not to hate her for interrupting our celebration.

When I saw the expression on her face though…something was wrong.

"It's the man you had us watch," she breathed. Poseidon tensed, eyes flicking uneasily to me. "You must come. Now."

I didn't even have time to open my mouth and ask what was happening before we flashed away.

"The bakery?" A sick feeling rolled through my gut as I blinked up at Silos' bakery. "You were watching Silos?" My words were a hoarse whisper. Poseidon didn't answer, just turned and followed Galatea toward the door. I hurried after them, fear spreading through me, as I glanced at the upper floor. *To the room where Lily was.*

The second I entered the bakery, my fear solidified into something much worse.

"Silos!" I ran forward, pushing past both Poseidon and Galatea, to where my friend was standing. "No!"

Stone. He was made from stone.

I was vaguely aware that there were more statues in the bakery, as though every one of his customers had also been turned to stone while he had been serving them.

My mind spinning, I raced for the door at the back, to the staircase.

I took the steps two at a time, bursting into Lily's room with a crash.

"Almi!" Poseidon's voice roared my name as the door slammed open.

Her bed was empty.

For a second, I couldn't breathe, my mind blanking completely.

I had been terrified of finding her as a statue, but not there at all?

"She's gone! Poseidon, she's gone!" I burst back into the bakery and froze.

Atlas was standing next to Silos' stone form, leaning against him like he was some sort of furniture.

"Where is she?" My words came out a scream, and Atlas laughed.

I looked at Poseidon, my eyes filling with angry, terrified tears. Unbridled fury filled his.

"The heart of a Nereid, huh?" Atlas said.

I'd thought I was already scared for my sister, but now I knew I was.

"You dare fucking touch her—"

He stepped forward, swiping his hand, and my threats fell away. I was moving my mouth, but no sound was coming out. Frustration made my entire body heat, and more furious tears streamed down my face.

"The thing is, Almi, Poseidon, and whoever the fuck you are,"—he said, waving a hand at Galatea—"you don't seem to understand the gravity of your situation. Almi, you especially, are under-informed." He turned his maniacal grin on me. "I've been on a little trip to see the Oracle."

"Atlas! We are mid-Trials, you can't interfere! What have you done with her sister?"

"I am not interfering. I am simply ensuring that I am in a fit state to rule your realm, when one of my minions win. By taking possession of the heart of the ocean. I assume, Almi, that he has told you the entire prophecy?"

I glared at him, and when that didn't feel like it expressed my feelings well enough, I spat at him.

His eyes darkened, and flames leapt up across his skin. "You're a vile little thing," he hissed. "I can see why he hid you away for so long."

"Why are you doing this now? Wait until the Trials are over, and I will face you one-on-one," Poseidon said.

"He knows you two will win," said Galatea, her voice loud and clear. I could have kissed her for the furious look her sentence brought to Atlas' face.

She was right. He was doing this because we'd just got so many shells.

Power erupted from him, a stream of fire slamming into Galatea. A wall of water burst up in front of her the same second it hit, dousing most, but not all, of the flames.

"Stop!" I screamed, visions of the bakery in flames rushing me. But no sound came out.

I ran at the Titan. He turned to me, his flames powering at me instead. But almost as though he was realizing an error, his face changed, and the fire vanished.

He began to laugh again. "No, no, no! I mustn't kill you! Death would be far, far too good for the wife of this monster." He turned to Poseidon, who hadn't moved. It finally occurred to me that that wasn't right, and I saw the strain in his body as he fought against some invisible force. Stone crept over his skin.

He was pinned by Atlas' power, just as I had been before.

"Where is Lily?" he ground out. Fresh tears started down my cheeks at hearing him say my sister's name.

"You want to find out? Forfeit your place in the Trials."

"I can't do that."

"Then her sister stays with me. I'm sure I can wed an unconscious sea nymph."

"I can't just hand over my realm to you."

Emotion was coursing through me. I knew Poseidon couldn't give up his realm. But how could he leave Lily in the hands of this monster?

There had to be another way.

Desperate words flowed from my lips, pleas and curses alike, but no sound came out. Hopeless frustration was causing a rage to build inside me like I had never felt.

"Then I keep the girl." Atlas shrugged his shoulders. "If your wife is of no further use to me, then perhaps it is time to repay the favor you did mine." Fire roared around him, and he turned to me.

"Atlas!" Poseidon roared, and I saw true fear in the sea god's face. Power exploded from him. I sent a desperate plea to the air to come and help me, to defend me from the maniac who had my sister.

And the air answered.

A fucking tornado burst to life before me, whipping around the gods flames and flinging them back at him. Atlas snarled as a tidal wave of water crashed over him. I screamed in dismay as the statue of Silos was knocked to the ground, along with all the other stone citizens in the bakery, and then the side wall of the building. Everyone froze for a split second as the building creaked, and I looked desperately at Poseidon.

Galatea ran to the middle of the room, her staff held high and glowing. A shield of water spewed from it as the building began to collapse around us, every statue safe inside it.

"You are pathetic!" Atlas cackled over the sound of crashing destruction. There was a flash of red, and then he was before me, his hand shooting out and gripping me by my neck. "Do you want to meet my wife, Almi? She's keen to meet you, I know." His breath seared my skin—it was so hot, and he was so close.

Air! Help!

The tornado slammed into us, knocking him sideways and dislodging his grip on my throat, and then Poseidon launched himself at the god. The two men rolled to the ground, water and flame crashing over them both as they fought.

"She's on her way!" Atlas yelled gleefully as he sprang to his feet. Poseidon landed his fist square in Atlas' face as he leapt up after him, and Atlas stumbled back, silver liquid running from his nose. His eyes turned completely black and when he spoke his voice was no longer his, but something out of a freaking horror film, so loud it sounded like it was coming from the earth itself.

"She's here. And she has your sister." He turned to me, his demonic eyes making my head spin and my stomach churn.

Lily was here?

"Do you want your sister back?"

Hope soared. "Yes!" My word actually sounded out loud, my voice returned. "Lily!"

"You'll need to convince my wife to give her to you."

I spun, looking for her. Golden snakes slithered toward us, through Galatea's shield of water. A hand pushed through the shield, green and long-fingered.

I heard Poseidon speak. "Almi, you have to go."

"What? No, not without Lily!"

"It's too dangerous."

I whirled to face him. "No! No, don't you dare take me from her again!"

"I'll get her back." His eyes were hard, filled with tortured emotion. "I promise."

I opened my mouth, but the world flashed white before I could say another word.

THANKS FOR READING!

Thank you so much for reading! If you enjoyed the second book of Almi and Poseidon's story, I would be so grateful for a review.

You can find the next book, Sacrifice of the Brave King, on Amazon.

You can get exclusive access to cut scenes and first looks at artwork and story ideas, plus free short stories and audiobooks if you sign up to my newsletter at elizaraine.com and you can hang out with me and get teasers, giveaways and release updates (and pictures of my pets) by joining my Facebook reader group, just search for Eliza Raine Author!